Everybody loves
the Last Kids on Earth series!

"TERRIFYINGLY FUN! Max Brallier's *The Last Kids on Earth* delivers big thrills and even bigger laughs." —JEFF KINNEY, author of the #1 *New York Times* bestseller *Diary of a Wimpy Kid*

★ "A GROSS-OUT GOOD TIME with surprisingly nuanced character development." —*School Library Journal*, starred review

★ "Classic ACTION-PACKED, monster-fighting fun." —*Kirkus Reviews*, starred review

★ "SNARKY END-OF-THE-WORLD FUN." —*Publishers Weekly*, starred review

"The likable cast, lots of adventure, and GOOEY, OOZY MONSTER SLIME GALORE keep the pages turning." —*Booklist*

"HILARIOUS and FULL OF HEART." —*Boys' Life*

"This clever mix of black-and-white drawings and vivid prose brings NEW LIFE TO THE LIVING DEAD." —Common Sense Media

Winner of the Texas Bluebonnet Award

MAX BRALLIER & DOUGLAS HOLGATE

VIKING

VIKING
An imprint of Penguin Random House LLC, New York

First published in the United States of America by Viking,
an imprint of Penguin Random House LLC, 2021

Text copyright © 2021 by Max Brallier
Illustrations copyright © 2021 by Douglas Holgate

Visit us online at penguinrandomhouse.com.

Library of Congress Cataloging-in-Publication Data is available.

Printed in the United States of America

ISBN 9781984835376

10   9   8   7   6   5   4   3   2   1

LSCH

Book design by Jim Hoover
Set in Cosmiqua Com and Carrotflower

For Alyse and Lila

—M. B.

For the Alice Miller

School Stick Fighting Club

VICTORIA NON SINE VULNERIBUS
"No victory without bruises"

—D. H.

I'm pumping gas into my BoomKart.
June's telling me there's no time.

And I know there's no time.

I know that the Mallusk—an enormous
centipede monster carrying the
Millennium Super Mall on its back—is
barreling toward us.

Man, I wish I could go back to three
minutes ago . . .

1

Three minutes ago, things were *good*! Me and my friends, Quint, June, and Dirk, were *good*!

We were mid–road trip and celebrating a hard-won victory at Aqua City water park. We had defeated the monster Blargus, survived Thrull's skeleton army, and escaped with Drooler. Drooler, the odd-looking little creature who secretes the strange liquid Ultra-Slime. And that strange liquid is, maybe, the key to defeating Thrull once and for all.

Yep, three minutes ago was a Kodak moment . . .

But then came the rumbling, like a thunderstorm giving birth to an earthquake.

The world started shaking. My insides started quivering.

Because we saw it . . .

"The Mallusk," June gasped. "It's back."

"Which means we gotta get back to driving," Dirk said. "And FAST."

So right now, my friends are in their BoomKarts, engines running. But I'm still pumping gas.

Actually, wait, no, I only *look* like I'm pumping gas. I'm actually just standing at the pump, in a half trance, staring at my hand. Not my normal hand.

The Cosmic Hand.

The Cosmic Hand is the sucker-covered monster-tentacle glove that is forever wrapped around my wrist and hand. Without it, I can't wield my baseball blade, the Louisville Slicer. And it's the Louisville Slicer that contains the power to command and control zombies.

I'm staring at the Cosmic Hand now—because I'm realizing it has *changed*. It looks more, I dunno, *substantial*. And it feels *different*.

And I think I know what caused this change . . .

Back at Aqua City, I did something *huge*. I controlled a zombie *without* the Louisville Slicer. For the first time ever, I controlled a zombie with *my mind* . . .

What was I *thinking*? Where did the idea to even *attempt* to control zombies with my mind *come from*?

The Louisville Slicer contains the power to control zombies, yes, but it works in a *very specific way*. I *say* the stuff I want the zombies to do, and then I swing the bat and the zombies do the stuff.

But it is NOT a "shut my eyes and think real hard with my *mind* and then talk to zombies with my *mind*" telepathy-type mind thing!

That it even *occurred* to me to try using my *mind* is just . . . *weird*! It'd be like sitting on the couch playing *Mario*, pounding the controller, and then thinking, "Hey, y'know what? Forget the controller! I'll just control Mario WITH MY MIND."

But that's what I did.

And it worked. I controlled a zombie with my mind.

And I *have* to tell my friends. "Guys! I didn't tell you! Back at the water park, I used, like, BRAIN POWERS to—"

"DUDE!" Dirk shouts. "DO YOU SEE THAT MALLUSK?? WE HAVE TO GO *NOW*!"

"But this is—"

SCREECH!

June peels out, leaving burnt rubber in her wake. She cuts the wheel, stomping the pedal, speeding toward me. "GET IN YOUR KART! AND DRIVE!" June barks.

"OK, fine, geez," I mutter. "Message received. Only had to say it once."

"NOW, JACK!" June orders—and this time I listen. The pump clangs to the ground as I jump behind the wheel of my BoomKart.

I wave the Louisville Slicer and shout a command to my zombies. "Alfred, Lefty, Glurm! Climb on!"

My zombie trio responds, hopping on the bumper and grabbing the BoomKart's rear cage. I stomp the gas and the tires scream. I'm speeding away from the station, following June, Quint, and Dirk out onto the interstate, as—

KAAAAAA-KRUNCH!!!

The sound of the Mallusk ramming into the gas station is like a sonic boom of annihilation, rocket-hurling our BoomKarts ahead.

"I'm trying to tell you something, guys!" I shout. "Something BIG."

"Not bigger than that!" Dirk barks, hooking a thumb at the Mallusk.

"Debatable!" I shout. "Bigger in size—well, duh, of course the Mallusk is bigger. But bigger in terms of, like, *impact. On us.* I'm not sure—"

"Jack, there is quite literally nothing that will have a bigger impact on us than that thing . . . when it impacts . . . ON US!" Quint shouts.

"Heads up!" June cries as the wide avenue narrows, shooting us onto a small-town main street. Dirk and June blast forward while Quint and I keep pace, side by side. We speed down post-apocalyptic streets, engines churning, keeping us just ahead of the charging Mallusk.

"Quint!" I shout. "We need to talk about what I did back at the water park! It was—"

"Incredible!" Quint exclaims.

"I know! *Thank* you! I mean, I controlled Alfred just by thinking about it! Dude, am I Jean Grey?"

"No, friend, not that. Look!" Quint says, lifting one hand from the wheel and pointing at Dirk, directly ahead of us.

Dirk's sword is slung over his back—and clinging to the sword's hilt is Drooler. Tiny droplets of Ultra-Slime fly off the monster.

"Forget Drooler!" I exclaim. "How are you *not* interested in the world-altering stuff that—"

"I am interested, Jack! I am incredibly interested in the world-altering stuff that Drooler is doing."

Just then, Dirk swerves to avoid a toppling streetlight. His Kart bangs into mine, and then he's speeding along beside us.

"Dirk!" Quint exclaims. "I've had the most incredible realization!"

"Me too," Dirk says. "I'VE REALIZED YOU TWO TALK WAY TOO MUCH DURING SPEEDING GETAWAYS! FOCUS ON STAYING ALIVE AND KEEP YOUR MOUTHS—"

"Closed!" Quint says. "A closed circuit! Combined, that's what Drooler and your sword form. That's why he hugs the hilt like that! Look! The Ultra-Slime seeps from Drooler, trickles down the sword, then flows back up into Drooler for reabsorption! Like electricity! Or evaportion!"

The Drooler + Sword Ultra-Slime Cycle

Dirk glances back at Drooler, over to Quint, then back at Drooler. Then—

"WHY DOES THIS MATTER RIGHT NOW?" Dirk shouts.

"Because scientifically—"

"I'M GONNA HAVE TO SEPARATE YOU THREE IF YOU DON'T STOP TALKING!" June shouts, throwing us a hard look over her shoulder. "Now, LISTEN. See that highway on-ramp up ahead? If we can get to that, we *might* escape the Mallusk and we *might* not die today!"

I squint. June's right—the looping ramp will carry us out of the Mallusk's path.

And that means . . . we'll survive!

And that also means . . . I'll be able to finish *one complete thought* without being interrupted by a lesson on "the science of Ultra-Slime"!

I smile. One day, this will all be a distant memory. A blip on the radar. A fun story we'll tell our robot grandkids . . .

And then, in an instant, it all falls apart.

Exhaust erupts ahead of me: June's BoomKart, belching smoke. Then Quint's and Dirk's Boom-Karts begin shuddering and shaking. Then my own engine rattles.

I glance down at the dash: gas tank is *empty*.

"Well, this is unfortunate timing . . ." Quint says.

The street sways and buckles. Pavement splits. Stores crumble. Streetlamps fall. I feel the sharp sting of concrete pelting me like a rubble rain shower.

The Mallusk's shadow falls over us. In moments we'll be guzzled up by this monster freight train . . .

"Seat belts tight!" Quint shouts.

"Keep arms, hands, and Droolers inside the vehicle at all times!" June says.

And try to remain alive, I think.

"C'mere, little dude!" Dirk says, reaching around to cradle Drooler.

"Alfred, Lefty, Glurm—hang on!" I shout. "This is gonna beeee—"

My words are drowned out as the sound of the monster's massive legs ripping apart the earth becomes a deafening roar.

My hands grip the wheel tight. I see it again: the Cosmic Hand, *changed*. And then all I see is darkness as the Mallusk rolls over us like an avalanche . . .

chapter two

It feels like the entire world explodes.

Any moment, I expect my body will break. First, there will be the impaling. Followed by the crushing. And then, finally, the liquefying.

But that doesn't happen.

I am neither impaled, crushed, or liquefied. Because we're not being run over—not *exactly*. Instead, we've been vacuumed up, into the darkness of the Mallusk's underside.

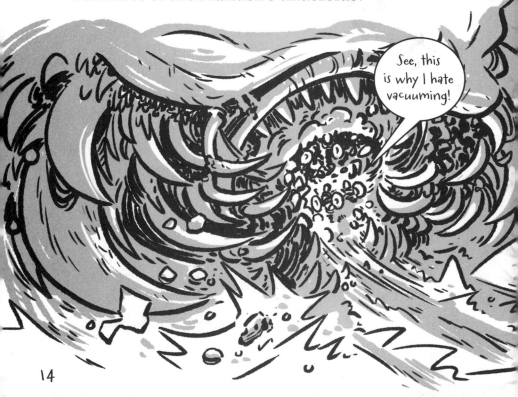

I quickly lose track of my friends—it's impossible to see anything but the millions of needle-like hairs that cover the Mallusk's massive pincer legs. I try to call out to them, but the instant I open my mouth, the air is *ripped* from my lungs. It's like I'm inside a tornado.

I faintly hear Alfred groaning. I squint back, just as he's yanked from the BoomKart and pulled into the swirling storm created by the rapid movement of the Mallusk's legs. Glurm and Lefty are snatched next, disappearing amidst the pounding pincers.

Then—

SNAP!

My seat belt pops and I'm hurled from the BoomKart! I'm suddenly like an astronaut, alone in space—only I don't have one of those neato cords tethering me to the ship. There is *zero* tethering happening here.

A tiny flicker of light, high above me, catches my eye. I realize I'm being hurled toward it with the Mallusk's every pulsating movement.

This is probably gonna not be great, I think as I'm propelled toward a pulsing hole that looks to be roughly the width of a Pringles can. The vacuum suction increases until—

FA-FOOM!

I'm shot through the hole, rocketed *out* of the world of Mallusk legs and pincers—and rocketed *into* something that looks and feels like lime Jell-O. My eyes are open, but the goo doesn't sting the way the chlorine in a motel swimming pool does.

I continue upward, through the Jell-O, blasting past . . .

Yum, Butterfinger!

I manage to twist in the green goo, avoiding a crunched-up, mangled gas pump—probably devoured moments earlier by the Mallusk, an unleaded afternoon snack. Then, finally, one last violent push and—

SPLOOSH!

My head and shoulders burst through the surface. After a quick gasp for air—

"JUNE! QUINT! DIRK!" I shout. "Where are you?"

The answer comes in the form of three sudden splashes. One by one, my friends erupt through the surface—gasping, coughing, spitting.

Well, that was a strange trip through a strange parfait.

I was thinking the same thing! But not parfait. I was thinking of the ice cream one. With the chocolate crunchies.

Carvel ice cream cake. The greatest of all cakes.

Enough with the cakes. I've got a problem.

"Dirk . . ." I start. I'm suddenly feeling sick—and it has nothing to do with the gallon of goo I swallowed. "Where's Drooler?"

Dirk's chin trembles as he looks at me. "I . . . I don't know. We got separated back there."

That's when I realize Drooler isn't the only missing member of our little adventure crew: my Zombie Squad isn't here, either. But I see the aching, awful look on Dirk's face—and I decide not to say anything. Alfred, Lefty, and Glurm are, y'know, *undead*—they could get pulled through a dozen Mallusks and be OK. They'll turn up. But Drooler? I'm not so sure.

"I held on to Drooler as tight as I could, and that's *really* tight," Dirk says. "But my sword got pulled away, so then he got pulled away, and now . . . Where is he?!"

I'm worried Dirk is going to go into full-on meltdown mode, until he adds, "I will personally punch every dumb pincer on this thing until I get Drooler back!"

That sounds more like the Dirk we know and love.

"Drooler must be somewhere," June says.

Quint nods. "We'll find him."

I wipe more goo from my eyes—and see we're in a dimly lit, cavernous chamber. Junk churns around us like we're in a garbage Jacuzzi. A mailbox bobs past us, followed by battered stop signs and deflated pool floaties.

"I think we were sucked up into the Mallusk's gastrointestinal tract," Quint explains as he paddles toward me. "Or some variation thereof."

"Lovely . . ." June says, flicking a fleshy gunk wad off her shoulder.

"Which means this, here, is the uprooted underside of the Millennium Super Mall," Quint says, pointing to the cracked concrete and jagged pipes that cover the ceiling. "The Mallusk's exoskeleton must have fused with—"

YEE-ARRRNK!

A monstrous bellow suddenly echoes through the chamber. "Watch out!" June cries.

She reels in the goo as a long, thick hose suddenly bursts out of the darkness!

"Whoa! Hose thing!" I cry, then—

SPLOOSH!

The hose stabs into the pool. Two more follow.

My friends and I are huddled together, nervously bobbing as the hoses poke around in the goo. Soon, each hose finds a piece of scrap, wraps around it, then pulls it from the pool.

"Those aren't hoses . . ." June says.

Our eyes have begun to adjust to the darkness, and it's clear they're actually the *trunks* of some strange new creature. And now those trunks are coming back, wrapping around us, hauling us away . . .

We are plucked from the goo-pool. One huge
elephant-like trunk swings, carrying us to a
platform at the pool's edge.

I feel like a 500-pound tuna that some happy
weekend fisherman just reeled in . . .

We are dropped—not gently—onto a pile of
junk. We're all dripping, head to toe, in a coat of
slime. We look like less famous, less successful
Ghostbusters.

Two squat monsters in clanging armor are
walking the platform, examining the newly
extracted junk. Which now includes *us*. "So, uh,
now what?" I whisper.

Just then, a voice—

"PSSST. This way!"

A small monster has just appeared in a
nearby doorway. I *almost* think I recognize the
creature, but I can't quite place it. The monster
beckons us, then disappears through the door. I
throw a glance back at the armored monsters—
then we all follow.

We turn the corner, into a dark hallway, and
June lets out a shriek. And that's when I realize
who this monster is.

June and Johnny Steve met out in the wilds, after she got separated from the rest of us. The pair embarked on their own adventure—leading a wingless baby Winged Wretch named Neon to safety. (Winged Wretches are usually evil—but Neon was good. Just goes to show: don't judge a creature by its species!)

"I didn't know if I'd ever see you again!" June says, overjoyed. She's swinging Johnny Steve around, hugging him tight: old friends together again.

Johnny Steve is beaming. "I was on the Mallusk's bow, sharpening my walking sword, when I spotted you four. So I hurried down here to be the very first to greet you!"

"Hey, Carmen Sandiego," I say, giving his trench coat a little tug. "Cool new clothes."

"Oh, yes," Johnny Steve says, and his eyes dart from side to side. "You see, I am a *spy* now—"

"Hey! The catching-up can wait," Dirk says. He turns to Johnny Steve. "Do you know where Drooler is?"

"What's Drooler?" Johnny Steve asks.

"You mean *who* is Drooler," Dirk says. "The answer is: only my favorite creature in the entire universe."

"And," I say, "if we want a real shot defeating Thrull and destroying the Tower, we need him."

"Also we need him, like, *emotionally*," Dirk adds. "And he needs me."

June kneels down to explain. "Dirk and Drooler were separated during that whole 'getting run over, flying through goo' process."

Johnny Steve fiddles with the collar of his trench coat for a moment, thinking. "In that case," he says, "Drooler will have been picked up by the Trawlsnouts by now—and given to the Junkers for delivery."

So *that's* what those elephant-trunk-like things are called: Trawlsnouts. And the armored dudes are Junkers.

"Whaddya mean delivery?" Dirk looks ready to fight some Trawlsnouts, some Junkers, and anything else thrown at him. "Delivery to *who*?"

"The Grand Protector, of course!" Johnny Steve says, like it's the silliest question anyone's ever asked. "*Everything* goes to the Grand Protector. And once the Grand Protector gets his claws on something he likes, he does *not* let go. I'm afraid, human pals, that there is no possibility of getting Drooler back."

chapter three

Dirk's not satisfied with Johnny Steve's answer—
not at all. So Johnny Steve begins leading us
through the maze-like depths of the mall,
toward the Grand Protector, and—hopefully—to
Drooler.

"So how'd you wind up on board this thing?"
June asks. "I wanna hear *everything*."

Johnny Steve beams. "Oh, it is a most
fascinating tale . . ."

"And that," Johnny Steve says, with a mournful sigh, "is how I learned it is a mistake to store one's collection of spectacles in the same bindle as one's collection of souvenir mugs."

"Does the Mallusk pick up *everything* in its way?" Quint asks.

"Nearly everything, yes," Johnny Steve replies. "The Mallusk seems to choose its path by somehow sensing where there are creatures in need. So some on board are weary, injured, or hunted . . . while others just happen to be in the right place at the right time. Like us!"

"Right place, right time," Dirk says. *"Right."*

"Hey, wait!" June suddenly exclaims. "Where's Neon? I'm gonna give him *so many scritches*."

Johnny Steve goes quiet and shifts uncomfortably. He tucks his walking sword under his trenchcoat, looking for any way to avoid June's gaze.

"Johnny Steve . . ." June says. Her voice is heavy now. "Tell me where Neon is."

Johnny Steve swallows. Then, finally, he says, "Well, uh . . . Neon exploded. Just . . . BOOM. He burst. Erupted. Like a water balloon."

"WHAT?!" June shrieks.

June has gone from "delighted to see you" to "ready to strangle you" real fast—and Johnny Steve knows it. "Truthfully, June," he says. "I do not know. Neon and I split up some time ago."

"But he was OK?" June asks. "When you last saw him?"

"Oh, most certainly!" Johnny Steve says.

"Not exploded?" June asks.

"Not exploded!" he answers happily. Then, quieter: "Neon had his own quest to attend to. Just as I am here, gone my own way, to be brave and do brave things—like a human!"

June blinks away any sadness about Neon. "This fight we're in . . ." she says quietly. "We each have to go where we're needed. I'll see Neon again, when it's time."

"And Jack," Johnny Steve says, turning the next corner, "I believe these three are with you."

"Alfred, Lefty, Glurm!" I exclaim. Relief fills me as I see my Zombie Squad. They are patiently waiting for me. A ton of fresh junk is hanging off them, including some pretty rad hats. They look like a so-bad-it's-good album cover . . .

"I knew you guys'd be OK!" I say. "C'mon, join up." And with a swing of the Slicer, I swoop them into a group, high-fiving each one as they fall in line behind us.

Dirk's walking faster now. I can see him losing patience. "So who's this 'Grand Protector'?" he asks. "What do I need to know?" I figure he's working on a strategy for Drooler's rescue, and, perhaps, Grand Protector punching.

"Auntie Anne!" Quint exclaims.

"Wait, the Grand Protector is Auntie Anne?" I ask. "The pretzel queen?"

"No! I *smell* Auntie Anne's pretzels!" Quint says. "Nearby."

Then we all smell the sweet sugar-salt scent. And it suddenly occurs to me that we haven't eaten in *way* too long.

In a flash, we're racing down the last corridor, giddy at the thought of cinnamon pretzel knots. Johnny Steve pushes open a heavy door and we're basked in a beautiful fluorescent glow. We gasp.

It is . . .

The Millennium Super Mall.

chapter four

"I knew the mall would be big," I say. "But I didn't know it would be *this* big."

It's so busy, my eyes don't know where to begin. This place is like a cruise ship's DNA was spliced with a creature carnival to create some massive mobile monster metropolis.

The mall's wide halls are busy thoroughfares, stretching off into the distance. And if what I'm seeing here is any indication of the mall's population, there must be *thousands upon thousands* of monsters aboard.

I can only hope they're friendly . . .

Dirk just asked the big question: the exact thing I was thinking. Four levels of monsters . . . They can't all be friendlies.

"Most everyone aboard is peaceful," replies Johnny Steve. "Mallusk City is a haven of sorts. A place for creatures who do not wish to involve themselves with events in this dimension or the larger war against Ŗeżżőcḥ."

"'Do not wish to involve themselves'?" Quint repeats.

"I didn't know not getting involved in the war was an option." I glance at my friends. "Did you guys know not getting involved in the war was an option?"

"Remember when you blew up Thrull's big Ŗeżżőcḥ tree, Jack?" Dirk says. "That's when it stopped being an option."

"Wait," June says. "What do you mean when you say *most* everyone on here is peaceful?"

"Sometimes . . ." Johnny Steve says mysteriously, "among the scents of giant cookies, Orange Juliuses, and deep-fried—"

Quint moans, "You're making me hungrier."

"Sometimes," Johnny Steve continues, "among those scents, I smell *evil*. I suspect I know which creature is emanating the smell, though I have yet to confirm my suspicions. However!" Johnny Steve pulls us close and uses his whispery spy voice. "I *will* figure it out. I am on board the Mallusk, *undercover,* keeping my ears open and an eye to the ground for anything that may help in the fight against Ṛeżżŏċħ!"

I feel like Johnny Steve's not a *great* spy if he just goes around talking about being a spy a whole bunch, but whatever. Plus, if you're gonna be a spy somewhere, this is not the worst place . . .

We pass a large fountain at one of the mall's many rotundas. It's now a hot tub. Monsters sit along the edges, sipping fizzy drinks and tossing a giggling Koosh-ball-type creature back and forth. I feel a sharp pang of loss—I want to sit in that hot tub and goof around with Bardle while Rover snores happily at the water's edge.

I'm suddenly yanked backward as Quint says, "Look where you're walking, Jack!"

"I totally am, what are you—"

ZOOM!

A two-car roller coaster rockets past me, zipping around a winding track so long it must stretch from one end of the mall to the other.

Inside each car is a rock-and-roll sorta monster, and they're engaged in something like a heavy metal showdown. Their instruments are standard Guitar Center stuff, but upgraded with other-dimensional modifications and alterations. These monsters are absolutely slaying—otherworldly shredding like nothing *anyone* has ever heard before.

As we continue through the mall, I can see June thinking. Wheels turning. "Johnny Steve," she says finally. "Are you *sure* these monsters won't join the fight against Thrull?"

"If it's not on this Mallusk, it's not their problem," says Johnny Steve.

And it seems like he's right. These creatures *do* behave differently from the monsters we've met before. A lumbering beast nearly crushes me, a school of snake-like creatures slither between my sneakers, and plenty of monsters look just as brutish as the ones at Chaz and Slammers—but not one of them threatens us.

The monsters that *look toughest* seem to be relaxing hardest. And the others are being busily industrious.

One thing is for sure: none of them are preparing for an epic battle to save the dimension.

"If these monsters won't fight, then we've got to move on," June says. "We need to be building an alliance to beat Thrull and getting to the Tower, not watching monster rock concerts. Let's find a way out of here."

"After we get our BoomKarts," Quint says.

"And Drooler," Dirk adds.

"And the fresh underwear," I remind them all. As the corridor widens, we enter a huge central square overflowing with activity.

"Ooh, look! Old Navy!" I say. "I wonder what the monsters turned *that* into."

"Board shorts!" shouts the reptilian creature outside the Old Navy. "Get your two-for-one board shorts!"

"Just Old Navy still," Quint says.

"AHHH!" June suddenly screams—a shriek so piercing I'm surprised it doesn't shatter every nearby storefront window. I spin, reaching for the Louisville Slicer, but instead of danger, I see . . .

THE VICTORY GEYSER!

"The Victory Geyser?" I ask, clueless.

"Yeah!" June says. "It's how they used to announce the *Late Teen Star* magazine Artist of the Year! I voted for the Big Haircut four hundred and ninety-seven times one year. Then my parents got a letter in the mail saying *Late Teen Star* magazine decided to limit voting to one vote per household."

I shrug. "What a bummer. I guess?"

June points excitedly. "And you see that big cannon-thing at the top? Each year, the Millennium Super Mall hosted the award show. Every thousand votes equaled one ballot ball. They dumped all the ballot balls in, live, on air. Once all the votes were in . . . BOOM! Harvey Cool Hair announced the winner and that geyser fired off a huge Silly String blast."

"It was terribly dangerous," Quint says, as we start down the next corridor. "They nearly had to cancel the awards altogether after a wayward Silly String blast almost brought down the Goodyear Blimp."

"It was rigged," June says. "In a fair election—"

"HEY!"

We all shut up and stare at Dirk. "I get it— this place is weird and whatever. But no more dilly-dallying . . . *we need to get back Drooler.*"

"You are in luck," Johnny Steve says. "We are nearing the Grand Protector's headquarters."

I glance up to the third level and see the mall's massive Food Court. It juts out, overlooking the mall below, like some sort of balcony a king would use to address his subjects.

"Oh!" Johnny Steve says. "As I said, the Grand Protector takes whatever he desires. And he *may* be interested in zombies. Jack, you might want to dismiss them."

Argh. I just almost lost my zombie buds! But I don't want whoever took Drooler to take them, too. So I say, "Zombie Squad, find a place to lay low," and with a wave of the Slicer I send them moving. They grunt and disappear inside Hot Topic. "Alfred better not come back with a pierced septum," I mutter.

"The Grand Protector's henchmonster is approaching," Johnny Steve whispers. "His name is Smud. He's delightful!"

Smud, a tall and beefy monster, is roller-skating out of an As Seen on TV store. And he definitely wasn't just browsing—he looks like he just glided out of an infomercial.

"Hey hey hey!" Smud says as he skids to a clumsy stop. "You must be the humans!"

"Are you the guy who's got Drooler?" Dirk demands. "The super-cute little creature?"

"No," Smud says. "I'm not really allowed near the valuable stuff. The Grand Protector has your friend."

Dirk's about to explode. "Then take me to this Grand Protector character . . . NOW."

"Well, this makes my job easy," Smud says. "Because the Grand Protector wants to see you . . . NOW." Then Smud glances at a clock on a mall directory. "Wait, wait, sorry. Not NOW. A little bit from now. It's Loot Day—and the Gifting of the Loot is about to begin."

Quint looks over. "Loot Day?"

June frowns. "Gifting of the Loot?"

Suddenly, a voice booms over the mall's public address system—those speakers that are usually announcing something like, "The mall will be closing in ten minutes. Please make your final purchases." And then everyone starts hurrying about, because even though you know it *probably* won't happen, there's this little thing in the back of your brain like, "Oh man, what if I don't make it out in time? Will I be trapped in the mall? I can't be trapped in the mall!" But also you secretly totally want to be trapped in the mall.

But what we hear over the PA system now is: "ATTENTION, CITIZENS! The treasures that the Grand Protector has discovered for you . . . will be distributed!"

It's like a switch has been flipped. All around us, monsters are hurrying to get a spot beneath the Food Court, turning it into a jam-packed mosh pit.

"Whoa," I say, glancing around. Monsters are amassing across the entire first level of the mall. "These guys love Loot Day, huh?"

A hush falls over the crowd. A figure is stepping to the Food Court's railing.

And when we see who that figure is, well, there's really only one reaction we can muster . . .

chapter five

"Evie Snark . . ." June growls.

"Oh, you know Evie??" Johnny Steve asks. "Well, that's nice. Friends, reunited!"

"Evie Snark is *not* our friend," I say. "She's the worst, and she's *out of her mind*. She stole the

Louisville Slicer! She caused Dirk to get bitten by a zombie! She summoned the Cosmic Terror Ghazt to our dimension!"

Looking up at Evie, I'm suddenly brought crashing back to that night at Dandy-Lions ice cream. The night Bardle died . . .

Evie helped awaken Thrull. And she stood there, did nothing, while Thrull killed Bardle.

Bardle might still be alive today if it weren't for her . . .

I shake away the thought. Need to focus on the here and now.

All around us, the monsters grow more and more eager for whatever is about to happen. Probably something self-important and annoying, if I know Evie.

She steps aside. "Presenting the one you've been waiting for, your beloved, the most benevolent, the Grand Protector . . . GHAZT!"

I gasp. Of course it's Ghazt!

The awful rat monster appears. "YES, IT IS I! GHAZT, THE COSMIC GENERAL!"

"I believe *that* may be the evil creature on board," Johnny Steve whispers.

"You're a great spy," June says, "because it *definitely* is."

I loathe Ghazt, but I gotta admit that he's looking good. Way better than the last time we saw him, swirling down a sewer pipe . . .

The New and Improved Ghazt, AKA Cosmic General, AKA the Grand Protector of Mallusk City

Shockingly defined biceps and forearms

Dream in eye?

New lease on life

"What are the odds that we'd wind up on the same mobile mall as those doofuses?" I moan.

"I'm looking forward to a rematch," Dirk mutters, glaring up at them.

Evie takes the PA microphone back and says, "GHAZT WILL NOW BESTOW UPON YOU MANY GIFTS!"

"Whoops! That's my cue!" Smud says. "I gotta help with Loot Day. Can't gift the Loot Globes without me!"

"Loot Globes," I say. "Sounds cool. Darn it."

Smud opens a gate that's been built around an escalator and quickly begins clomping upstairs. "I'm coming! I'm coming! Don't start yet!"

Dirk darts forward, trying to follow, but—

SLAM!

Smud is barely two steps up the escalator when the gate clangs shut. It sparks, electricity running through it. I notice the same electrified protection runs around the entire Food Court, keeping everyone but the Grand Protector and his friends out.

Smud makes it upstairs to the Food Court and speeds behind Ghazt, out of sight.

Evie announces, "AND NOW . . . GRAND PROTECTOR, PLEASE PULL THE LEVER!"

Ghazt looks sort of bored by this whole thing, but Evie gives him a little elbow to the rear, and he delivers his next line. "IT IS BY MY PAW THAT YOU ARE GIFTED THESE LUXURIES! IT IS BY MY PAW THAT YOU ARE KEPT SAFE!"

Ghazt slaps awkwardly at the lever while Evie scowls. Finally, he gets his paw around it, and—

KSHH-HISSS!

The mall's monorail slides into view behind Evie and Ghazt.

Smud hurries to get on board before it takes off again. He just barely makes it, scrambling in as it glides away from the Food Court, out over the mall.

The monorail car is jammed full of round containers, like giant plastic Easter eggs: the "Loot Globes."

"What's in those?" Quint whispers.

We don't have to wonder for long. Evie's voice booms: "AND NOW . . . THE GIFTING BEGINS!"

With that, Smud kicks the first plastic Loot Globe overboard. It breaks open midair and . . .

SMASH!

"Are these all items that the Mallusk picked up?" Quint asks.

Johnny Steve nods. "Yes. After the Trawlsnouts collect them and the Junkers sort them, the Grand Protector distributes them among the citizens of Mallusk City. He is quite generous."

The monorail car winds through the mall, with Smud steadily kicking the plastic Loot Globes over the side.

The monsters don't fight over the stuff that falls out. No weapons are drawn. When one monster gets something another wanted, a trade is quickly worked out.

The monorail heads deeper into the mall, following the long, curving track. When it finally returns, all the Loot Globes are gone— and the citizens of Mallusk City are content.

"I think the party's just about over," June whispers as the car begins gliding back into the Food Court station.

"NEVER FORGET WHO GRANTED YOU THESE GIFTS: I, YOUR GRAND PROTECTOR!" Ghazt shouts. He flips a lazy wave at the monsters below, then disappears back into the Food Court.

The monsters cheer, but I notice they don't seem 100 percent into it. It's more like a school assembly, where your teacher tells you ahead of time that you *have* to clap for the guest speaker . . . *or else.*

"We'll be back for Loot Day, same time next week!" Evie shouts into the PA.

Then Evie's gaze swings down, sharp, staring at us. Staring at ME. And—

CLANK!

The armored gate around the escalator swings open again, and Smud totters out on his skates. "The Grand Protector will see you now! Are you excited? I bet you're excited."

"Good luck," Johnny Steve whispers.

Dirk and I exchange looks. My buddy is a boxy bundle of barely suppressed rage—focused only on getting Drooler *now*. And my teeth are clenched like a vise, knowing I'm about to see Evie, up close, for the first time since Dandy-Lions. Since Bardle died.

My heart is *thump-thump*ing as we follow Smud up the long escalator to Evie and Ghazt's headquarters. As we get closer to the top, I feel the Cosmic Hand begin to gently, subtly pulse . . .

chapter six

The moment I see Evie, my body starts to tremble. I take slow breaths, trying to calm myself—but the calm isn't coming.

Watching her power-mad, mock-generous loot monologue was bad. This is worse.

Evie says, "I'm trying to remember . . . when did we last see each other? Oh, right! The ice cream shop. If I recall, Jack, you were sitting on your butt while your old wizard friend *died*."

Her words hit me right in the gut. I move so instinctively that it takes me a moment to even realize what I'm doing: reaching over my shoulder for the Slicer.

The blade is within my grasp, and I feel the Cosmic Hand *tug*, like a magnet held close to the fridge. My fingers spread wide, about to grab the handle, when—

"We're here for Drooler," Dirk says. His voice is steady, but the demand is clear. "Give him."

"Ehhh, sorry, not gonna happen," Evie says with a mocking little smile. "But I can *show* you your little friend."

Evie punches a button and a Sbarro security gate lifts open. And there he is: Drooler, inside a cage. A *strange* cage. It looks like an otherworldly, monster version of some case where museums keep million-dollar diamonds.

"DROOLER!" Dirk says. "You OK, buddy?"

Drooler squeaks happily, totally oblivious to the high-stakes happenings around him. That's a relief, and it allows Dirk to calm down a tiny bit.

Ghazt reaches down and scoops a pawful of Ultra-Slime from a puddle beneath Drooler's cage. Ghazt gestures with the slime, like some supervillain trying to show off his cool new toy. But he's clumsy and accidentally smears a bunch on his fur.

His paw sticks to his fur. He tugs. Still stuck.

We all watch as this great, powerful, Cosmic Warlord struggles to separate paw from fur. When he finally does, there's a Velcro-type ripping sound and a tuft of hair comes with it, leaving a not-great-looking bald spot.

AHEM. FEAR ME.

Ghazt collects himself and goes on. "This Ǧhṛužǧhŭt Spit—or Ultra-Slime, as you call it— is the substance best able to destroy the vines spreading across your ugly little dimension."

Evie grins. "That's why *we* are watching over 'Drooler.' Or, I mean, Ghazt is, rather. He's the Grand Protector. So he is *protecting* Drooler."

"*You're trying to tell me that weird cage is for Drooler's protection?!*" Dirk says.

"Exactly!" Evie says. "You get it. It's a classic protection cage. So, nope, you can't have him back. Grand Protector privileges. The Grand Protector gets first dibs on everything brought on board the Mallusk. That's just how it is."

I lean toward Quint and quietly whisper, "Why are they so into the Ultra-Slime? What do they care about destroying Thrull's vines? I mean—that's sort of *our* thing."

Apparently my quiet whisper wasn't quiet enough, because Ghazt roars, "Thrull STOLE MY POWER! He stole my tail, and with it, my ability to command the undead. That's why I must FIND Thrull and DEFEAT him! I will GET MY POWER BACK. I will show him NO MERCY and he will feel SO MUCH PAIN. SO MUCH!"

My face pales. Because, of course, that's not

true. Ghazt only *thinks* Thrull has his power.

The person who *actually* has Ghazt's power? It's me. The power is right here, in the Slicer, just a few Food Court tables away from Ghazt.

Quint is looking at me hard—shooting me the type of eye-beam stare that can only be exchanged between two best friends that have been through serious stuff. The eye-beam stare says a ton without saying anything at all . . .

Best friend eye-beam stare*

*QUINT'S EYE BEAM: They have no idea that *all* of Ghazt's power resides in the Midnight Blade. They've only seen you do one minor zombie-controlling trick at the bowling alley. We mustn't let them know. No matter what, you *cannot* use the blade in their presence.

"Um, uh, well then," I say, trying hard to avoid looking at or even thinking about the Slicer. "It sure is a good thing that no one on this mall has your tail powers, Ghazt. Sure is."

I stuff one hand in my pocket and try to casually look away, hoping Ghazt hasn't caught on. And that's when I notice just how jam-packed this place is with loot.

Up here, seeing what goes on inside their headquarters of evil, it's clear: everything truly valuable that the Mallusk vacuums up, Ghazt and Evie keep for themselves . . .

Smud is sorting through new loot as we talk. Some goes into a pile for Gifting Day, but the primo stuff goes into a separate pile for Evie and Ghazt. A busted lawn chair is tossed into the Gifting Day pile, but a ten-foot-tall model of the Incredible Hulk goes into Evie's pile.

It's so bogus! I'm mad on behalf of the mall monsters. What if one is a big Hulk fan, huh?

"Question," June says. "Ghazt, if you want to get your tail and power back from Thrull so bad, what are you doing cruising around on a mall? Shouldn't you be heading straight to the Tower?"

"Oh, they don't know where the Tower is!" Smud happily calls from his loot-sorting post.

"Smud," Evie growls. "SHUT. UP."

"Sorry," he says meekly. "I just wanted to be part of the conversation."

I try to keep a poker face. My friends are doing the same. But it's not easy, because we know two *big* things that these guys don't. We know that I have Ghazt's powers, *and* we know where the Tower is.

"I do so know where the Tower is," Ghazt says. "Generally. Mostly. I know the direction! The Tower is *mine*, and it beckons me."

"Riiight. Gotcha," June says. "So the Tower is, like, 'You're getting warmer. Warmer. Oh, no, colder now.' Wow—that's *some cosmic power.*"

OK, I'm starting to get their strategy.

First, I understand why Ghazt wants Drooler—the little guy is the best possible weapon for destroying Thrull.

Second, I understand the value of the mall. They're picking up tons of stuff and monsters—and anything they grab could offer a clue to the Tower's location.

The one thing I *can't* figure out? How to use any of this to rescue Drooler.

Suddenly, from the courtyard below, we hear: "CANNONBALL!"

We peer over the railing just in time to see a monster leaping off the awning of the Lego store and splashing into a fountain.

In a flash, Evie is marching to the railing in full-on bad-mood lifeguard mode. "YOU DOWN THERE! Have you forgotten Grand Protector Law #19? No horseplay in the fountains!"

The monsters grumble. One angrily punctures her inner tube with her horn and it deflates with a sad hissing sound.

Ghazt sighs. Evie smiles.

I make note of all this. Ghazt may have declared himself "Grand Protector," and Evie may be *very* happily enforcing random rules, and the monsters might appreciate the safety of having a Cosmic General on board . . . But as leaders, these two don't appear to be particularly beloved.

"Look." Quint nods to the surrounding walkways. Evie's scolding has attracted a crowd. And that crowd has caught sight of our Food Court standoff. Monsters are gathering at every level, watching us.

"Evie, I can't help but notice that your rules," June says, "they seem a little . . . dumb."

"No horseplay in the fountains is not a rule!" Evie snaps. "It is a LAW."

"Are those . . . two different things?" I ask.

"Yes! There is only *one rule* aboard this mall!" Evie yells, pointing to the wall. "THAT ONE! READ THE SIGN!"

"Shoplifters will be prosecuted?" I ask.

"Sunday is half-priced appetizers at the Rainforest Café?" June tries.

Evie is about seven seconds from exploding, but she manages to catch herself. "This discussion is pointless," she says. "It's very simple. Ghazt is the Grand Protector of this city. If you're not the Grand Protector—or not very close personal friends with the Grand Protector—then what you say doesn't matter."

"And who elected you guys Grand Protector?" June asks.

"No one," Evie says. "Ghazt is a Cosmic General—a natural-born leader. The monsters flock to his power. And mine, too, a little. A LOT. Even more than Ghazt. No, about the same. Or maybe I'm—"

I shoot a quick look at June. I see wheels turning. But before she can say what she's thinking, Dirk *roars*—

"ENOUGH! I don't care about your rules, your laws, or any of that junk. I promised to take care of Drooler—and that's what I'm gonna do."

An awful, knowing grin appears on Evie's face. "You are welcome to try," she says as Dirk stomps past her.

Dirk unballs his fists and reaches for the cage. I feel a shudder and quake ripple through the Mallusk, and then—

"As I said, you cannot have him," Evie says
gleefully. "You cannot *take* him. As long as the
mall is under our control, Drooler is ours."

Dirk rises. He's mad. Like, ear-smoking,
eyeball-popping, fireball-in-your-chest furious.

"OK," June says, raising her arm and pulling a
lever on Blasty. "I think *now* the fight happens."

"Was hopin' you'd say that," Dirk says.

"I concur," Quint says, raising his staff. "Actually, let me clarify. I concur that I think a fight will probably now happen. I do not concur that I was hoping June would say that."

"I knew what you meant, bud," I say.

Evie flashes an eager smile—and I swallow. To be honest, I'm not super keen to rumble with these two. I mean, Ghazt's got his new buff bod, and I can't sic my zombies on him without him realizing I'm the one who has his powers. And sure, he may have taken the form of a rat—but that rat is roughly the size of a rhinoceros.

But before the fisticuffs can even begin, a distant thunderclap sound stops us in our tracks.

And then a howl: the most spine-chilling sound I've ever heard.

And then, at once, from everywhere, monsters are shouting.

No, not shouting. *Screaming* . . .

chapter seven

The howl grows louder—a piercing cry that
penetrates the walls of the mall.

A monster cries out, "Up there! Outside!"

Another monster yells, but I can't make out
the words. The howl is too loud now, too close. It
builds and builds until—

BOOM!

A shock wave explodes through the mall,
ripping down the long corridors. The Mallusk
rocks and reels, like a pirate ship suddenly
struck by enemy artillery.

I whirl around—and see Evie, Ghazt, and
Smud fleeing.

"Kids, it's been nice catching up! But we gotta
go!" Evie calls as they race to the rear of the
Food Court.

"Some 'Grand Protector,'" June mutters.

At the far wall, Evie yanks a lever, then—

KLANG!

Steel security gates drop from the ceiling! They spark and sizzle—electrified, like everything else up here. The gates have divided the Food Court into two—and we're on the side without Drooler. Evie throws us a final glance—

then the lights flicker and everything on their side of the gate is hidden in darkness.

"Guess we'll have to consider that fight 'to be continued,'" June says.

Behind us, the door to the escalator swings open. Another shrieking howl from outside— followed by another BOOM. The floor ripples beneath us.

"Rippling floors are probably a cue to leave," I say.

"Indeed," Quint agrees.

"Drooler! I'll get you of there! Somehow!" Dirk calls. "Promise!"

Drooler squeaks, still oblivious. We race up the escalator, then out onto one of the third level's wide halls. We're immediately swept up in a tangled wave of fleeing bodies—the monsters are one terrified, surging mass.

I manage to grab the arm of a hunched, needle-backed monster. "What's happening?!" I ask.

"I do not know!" the monster shrieks. "The Mallusk has never been attacked! That is why—"

SHRREEEEEEEEEEEEE!

Another high-pitched, wind-torn howl slices through the mall. It pierces my ear drums. Monsters cover their ears, earholes, ear-balls, and any other ear-like body parts.

The howl grows louder, louder, louder, until—

SKKKRUCH!

"Watch out!" June barks, and the Mallusk reels as a giant, monstrous *blade* bursts through the wall!

Dazzling bright daylight pours in as the monstrous blade opens up the mall like it's performing brutal battlefield surgery. The blade smashes apart stores, shatters glass elevators, splits open ceilings.

Monsters are slithering, scrambling, and springing for cover. Some slam doors to bathrooms and stores, locking themselves in. Others dive into kiosks like they're foxholes.

"Guys," I say. "I think we gotta go to the roof."

"Hate to say it," June says, "but I agree."

"Yep," Dirk says, glancing around. "These monsters here—they're not gonna fight."

"To the escalator!" Quint says, leading the way. "Quickly!"

Shouldn't this be Evie and Ghazt's job?

The so-called protectors are off protecting themselves.

Both sides of the escalator are flooded with monsters heading down, hoping to find safety on the lower levels. We're like fish trying to swim upstream—*toward* the danger, rather than away from it.

"Up the middle!" June says, as she dodges a monster's swinging tail, then leaps onto the escalator's metal divider.

We reach the mall's top level. We push through a maintenance door, speed up a cold cement stairwell, then finally burst outside.

And I instantly regret my "go to the roof" suggestion.

Monstrous howls fill the dusk sky like air-raid sirens, and I swallow a meatball-sized lump in my throat.

KRAK

The horrible noise pierces the air every time they dive. And as one zooms overhead, I see why: the monsters' wide, leathery wings have thin tears in them. The air rushing through the tears creates the spine-chilling howl.

"They're dive-bombing the mall!" Quint yells. "Using their ax-tails to cut it apart."

"Won't be long until the mall's just a whole bunch of rubble," Dirk says.

One passes directly overhead, and I get a clear view of the monstrous species known as—

-HOWLER!-

Howling wing slits

Jaw like a Venus fly-trap

Double-sided ax-tail

Scaly reptilian skin

The swarming Howlers circle up to begin another round of low-flying, torpedoing attacks.

One speeding Howler momentarily blocks the blinding sun, and I can see clearly into the distance. There's some sort of national park or nature reserve ahead, towering trees packed together so tightly they almost form a ceiling.

"If the Mallusk can reach those trees, the howlers might have to retreat," Quint says.

June says, "So we just have to hold them off until we reach the tree line."

"Great!" I say. "June, use Blasty to shoot them all down!"

"ARE YOU KIDDING? I have a tiny little-gadget cannon thing here. Not that thing from *The Ninth Neutron* or whatever that movie is you and Quint are always yakking about."

"*The Fifth Element.* And point taken."

KRUNCH!

An ax-tail slices through an air-conditioning unit, kicking up a massive cloud of dust that swirls around us—and causes June to smile . . .

"OK, I can't blast them down," June says,

jamming her hand into her pocket and pulling out a fistful of Goober Gag smoke spheres. "But I *can* make it hard for them to see!"

As June jams the smoke spheres into Blasty, I spot a swooping Howler—and use the Slicer to point out the target.

Clouds of blue and orange smoke quickly fill the sky. One Howler bursts through the smoke— then curves away, confused. Purple smoke erupts, and another blinded Howler is forced to peel off.

It feels like we're playing a video game: June is the one with the controller, and we're the lousy players on the couch, doing our part by calling out any bad guys she might miss.

"Forty-five degrees to the right!" Quint yells.

"On it!" June barks, firing.

The smoke sphere explodes in a cloud of green. The Howler rips through it, spinning, momentarily disoriented. Then—

KRRRUNCH!

The mall's sky-scraping radio tower erupts as the Howler smashes into it! The monster shrieks as jagged metal tears a gaping hole in its left wing. It's off-balance now, dropping quickly, unable to stay upright with one working wing.

And that puts it on a collision course with Quint.

"Buddy, watch out!" I cry, but he can't hear me over the monster's deafening shriek.

In moments, the monster will smash into Quint. I jam the Slicer into its sheath and start sprinting.

I need to tackle Quint. Get him down before the Howler *takes him down.*

But I'm not going to reach him in time. The angle's all wrong. So as the Howler flashes in front of me, I spring into the air, my hand outstretched—*the Cosmic Hand outstretched.*

I don't know where the idea comes from, but something inside of me is saying that if I could just grab hold of the Howler . . . I could yank it to a halt, rip it out of the sky, and then fling the beast like a Frisbee.

It's an impossible idea. But somehow, in that moment, the idea seems 100 percent doable.

My fingertips brush against the speeding Howler's hanging talon. My hand swipes at the scales covering its cold, iridescent underside. My palm grazes the Howler's trailing tail.

Then, just before my fingers meet the beast's double-blade ax, the Cosmic Hand's suckers *stick*. Pain explodes in my arm, like it's just been jerked from my shoulder, Wookiee-style.

Yep, that idea was 100 percent *not* doable.

The Cosmic Hand tightens around the tail and I feel a surge of energy. A flurry of fantastical images and cacophonous cries cascade through me—jumping from the Howler into the Cosmic Hand, then rushing up into my brain-parts. Everything goes dark, and then suddenly . . . Suddenly I *see*.

It's like I'm peeking behind the curtain—seeing what isn't supposed to be seen. I *feel* the uncaring evil of the Howler. I *hear* distant words, spoken in the language of Ṛeżżőcħ.

It lasts only a moment—and then the Cosmic Hand loosens and my eyes flash open.

The Howler is staring at me. There's a nightmarish moment where I think the monster's face has turned haunted, demonic—then I realize it's only that I'm seeing its face upside down. Because *I'm* upside down.

The Howler's eyes bore into me, something like *knowing* in them.

I try to squeak out something like, "Could you keep your eyes on the road, please?" but the crashing wind shuts me up. The Howler flies lower, faster, taking me on a rocket-speed death-ride toward the front of the Mallusk.

So I open my hand. I let go . . .

The air explodes from my lungs as I slam to the roof. My body skips across the mall's surface like a stone flung over water.

I tumble into a sitting position, head spinning. I shake away the dizziness—just in time to see the Howler blast ahead of the Mallusk.

I stand.

My first few steps feel like I'm walking on a half-busted air mattress. But the next few are more stable, and I'm running nearly steady by the time I reach the mall's front end, where there's nothing below but Mallusk.

The loudest howl yet cuts through the sky. The Howler is rocketing back toward the mall. Toward me.

Its eyes catch mine, and there's something like cruel, cunning *satisfaction* in them. Its wings snap tight against its body, making it look like some sort of supersonic drill-blade.

It angles down.

Picks up speed.

And hurtles itself headlong into the Mallusk! Everything shudders as the Howler slams into the spot between the Mallusk's front horns like some sort of self-destructive death-torpedo—

Bits of flesh fly. A sudden shower of scales and splintered wing-bone. The Howler is gone. He must have exploded against the surface, then been pulled under the Mallusk and crunched beneath the weight of the beast.

The Mallusk roars in pain. The sound is almost mechanical—a gruff, engine-grinding wail. She's hurt—and hurt *bad*. Her head sways from side to side and she speeds ahead faster.

"We're at the trees!" Quint shouts.

I drop onto my stomach as the Mallusk charges into the tree line. The remaining Howlers are forced to retreat as the the towering forest becomes a protective canopy.

I let out a deep breath. We made it. We're safely hidden beneath the trees, where no Howler can reach us—

SKREEE!

OK, where *one* Howler can reach us. The lone remaining monster is missing one wing, too injured to take flight. But not injured enough to call it quits . . .

The monster begins stomping across the mall, its dragging ax-tail shredding the roof.

I race back toward my friends.

"Not looking great!" I say as I reach them.

"Nope," Dirk says. "It might as well be tucking a napkin into its neck."

I suddenly know what a gazelle must feel like, caught in the open savannah by a hungry lion.

We take a step back—and there's a sound like ice splintering. I look down—and my head goes all spinny and swimmy.

We're standing atop the atrium's huge domed skylight—and the glass is breaking.

A fracture in the smooth surface is spreading out, looking like the crisscrossing highways on Dirk's road trip map.

Far, far below us, I see the mall's shiny tile floor.

"DON'T!" June cries as the Howler takes another step forward. "NO FARTHER!"

"I DOUBT YOU UNDERSTAND!" Quint shouts. "BUT THIS WILL BE *BAD*! FOR ALL OF US!"

The Howler ignores their words—until it takes its first step onto the glass. It must sense the danger then, because it freezes. And now all five of us are just standing still as the jagged cracks fan outward, farther and farther.

It's gonna happen. It's gonna fully shatter. And I'm way behind on my levitation lessons . . .

CRICK-CRIIIIICK-
CRAAAAAAACK!

KRRRRIIISSSSSSHHHHH!!

chapter eight

The skylight erupts in a million tiny shards, glass exploding around us like diamond confetti. The Howler plunges through—and my friends and I follow . . .

My stomach does a roundoff, full-twisting, back-handspring layout that would for sure get me a perfect ten from any judges. But there are no judges—just hundreds of monsters, watching from every level of the mall. All eyes (and other optical orifices) are locked on us, as—

SLAM!

The Howler hits the floor like a bowling ball dropped onto concrete from a hundred stories up. I hit next—and I get lucky. I land on the one spot on the Howler's body not covered in armored scales: its belly.

It's like a trampoline . . . sorta. Difference is, when you land on a trampoline you don't feel bone or muscle or what might be a spleen underneath. I mean, I'd hope. If you do, you got yourself a creepy-weird trampoline and you should probably see about getting a refund.

"HEADS UP!"

I throw myself to the side as Dirk lands next, turning the Howler's bare gut into something like one of those inflatable blob-thingies at summer camp. Y'know, those things where one kid jumps and then the other kid is catapulted into a lake? It's like that . . .

I get lucky *again*—launched toward the fountain, landing with a hard *SPLASH*. But it's not water in the fountain. I'm smacking my lips, trying to pin down the strange flavor when—

SLAM! SLAM!

June and Quint hit the Howler's belly at the same moment. Then, together, June and Quint and Dirk are launched off the Howler's gut. They're tumbling through the air, then—

We burst through the surface, and Quint's already pointing, planning. "It's hurt! Look!"

A large, open wound is visible on the Howler's side—and the unmistakable stench of evil wafts off it. It stinks like a back-alley dumpster.

The Howler lets out a throat-shredding shriek of rage, then rises—jaws snapping, tail swinging, talons digging into the cracked floor.

"Bad news, gang," I say. "I think he likes grape soda."

"Well, he can have it," June says. We all slip and splash and fumble out of the fountain, just seconds before—

KRAKA-SMASH!

The Howler explodes *through* the fountain! Over the sound of bursting concrete and splashing grape soda, I hear a voice—a voice I haven't heard once during this entire attack.

"Hey! That's what *I* was gonna say!" June growls.

Quint immediately understands what Evie's up to—and he's *mad*. "Evie's loudly broadcasting combat strategies to make it appear as if *she's* figuring out how to save everyone. Instead of us!"

"ANY MOMENT, THESE INNOCENT MONSTERS WILL BE SLAUGHTERED!" Evie shouts. "PLEASE, JACK, YOU SNIVELING COWARD! STOP BEING A SNIVELING COWARD AND DO AS I SAY! YA COWARD."

My jaw cracks in anger. I'd like to climb up to Evie's cozy Food Court fortress and give her a piece of my mind. Not an important piece, like all the stuff you need to do to finally get the Biggoron's Sword in *Ocarina of Time*. Some piece of my mind I *don't* use. State birds or something.

"Car!" Quint suddenly cries, pointing. "Big car! Big car incoming!"

The Howler's ax-tail has just sliced through a fancy velvet-rope barrier and smacked the slick silver convertible behind it. The car's alarm blares as it spins in the air, flipping, sailing straight toward us.

"After you!" I shout, and we all race after
Dirk, following him into the matress store. And
not a moment too late. The convertible SLAMS
into the entrance behind us—and the Howler
follows it.

We duck down behind a huge bedroom set.
Pillows and blankets are piled high everywhere,
keeping us hidden—for now—from the stalking,
searching, *hunting* Howler.

"Sure could use some help from the locals," Dirk grunts angrily.

"Don't hold your breath," I say. "These mall monsters aren't going to get involved as long as Evie and Ghazt tell them that they have it all under control. Problem is, Evie and Ghazt *don't* have it all under control!"

"So we do the very thing I was *gonna* say we do, before Evie went and shouted it everywhere," June says as she spins a dial on Blasty. "We go for the wound."

"Problem," Quint says. "The Howler is quite colossal. Reaching the wound will be difficult."

June flashes a mischievous grin. "What, you never got in trouble for jumping on the bed?"

"Trouble? No," Quint says. "In fact, my parents encourage energetic—"

"Not now, dude," Dirk says, as he grabs a standing lamp. I draw my Slicer while Quint readies his staff.

"OK," June breathes. "On my signal—"

"THE MONSTER IS A THREAT TO THE MALL'S FINE CITIZENS! DESTROY IT!" Evie bellows. "GO FOR THE WOUND!"

"Ugh, yes, I was about to say that!" June cries. "Stop taking our ideas and acting like they're your ideas, Evie!"

"Uh, hey, June," I whisper. "I don't think Evie can hear you . . ."

"Shut up, Jack."

And that's the signal. The words "Shut up, Jack" are barely out of June's mouth when we burst out into the open, each of us racing toward a bed, and then leaping, launching upward—

The Howler's pained shriek could move mountains. Its head bangs *hard* into a ceiling fan. Its eyeballs rotate clockwise. And finally—

WHOMP!

The Howler crashes into a bunk bed, smashes through it, then lands belly up. A long gray tongue tumbles out of its mouth, flopping onto the floor with a wet smack.

And finally, it's quiet.

"Guess he was tuckered," I say. "*Dead tuckered.*"

June groans. Dirk groans louder. "Close enough, friend," Quint chuckles.

"Thanks for the support, buddy," I say as I plant my foot on the Howler's chest.

Wait, Jack. Move your foot!

But I'm doing a heroic monster-slayer pose! You guys can do it, too, there's plenty of room.

I'm confused why you're not right now, to be honest.

June grabs my ankle and yanks me down.
That's when I see what has Quint so intrigued.

There is something like a necklace around the
Howler's neck, except it definitely isn't, like, his
grandma's pearls.

I peer closer. The whole necklace sort of
intertwines with the Howler's scaly skin.

"It's almost like . . . a mark," June says. "Or
a symbol."

"It's Thrull," Quint says, plucking a chunk of it, which momentarily writhes in his hand like a snake. "These are Thrull's vines."

"Thrull's making more progress by the minute," June says. "His forces go way beyond a skeleton army now."

"But what are those forces doing attacking a big mall?" Dirk asks.

"Perhaps it is not the mall he wants," Quint says. "Perhaps it is us."

"Oh yeah, he for sure *does* want us," I say. "But how would he even know we're here? It's gotta be something else . . ."

"Probably the two-for-one board shorts," Dirk says.

Suddenly there's a loud stomp from deeper within the store. We all whirl, and—

"Ghazt," I growl.

The hulking rat beast stalks toward us, smacking aside dressers and nightstands, before finally stopping at the Howler. He bends over the fallen beast and—

CHOMP!

Ghazt's teeth plunge into the Howler's armored neck scales, like he's some sort of Dracula rat.

"I think you should know," Quint tells Ghazt urgently, "these flying beasts are in league with Thrull. They wear his vines. We don't know why—but if his forces are targeting the Mallusk, then the monsters here need to prepare to defend themselves and their home."

Ghazt acts like Quint isn't even speaking. He just swaggers out of the store, the limp Howler hanging from his teeth.

"What the huh?" I say. We all exchange confused glances, then follow Ghazt out to the main concourse.

Ghazt drops the Howler onto the floor. The beast is splayed out for all to see. The monsters cheer! Then Evie's voice booms—

FRIENDS! MONSTERS!

Today is an auspicious day. Ghazt the Cosmic General has done what Jack Sullivan and his friends could not! He has single-handedly slayed the beast that assaulted our home! Ghazt—and Ghazt alone—is truly your Grand Protector!

SKRIT SKRIT

chapter nine

Unbelievable! Evie and Ghazt are trying to take credit for *us* defeating that Howler!

"Let us all remember the great risk at which Ghazt placed himself," Evie says as she makes her way back up to the Food Court. "We are alive now because of his fearless bravery and leadership. That's why he is . . . your GRAND PROTECTOR!"

I glance sidelong at my friends. The same look is plastered across each of our faces . . .

This look!

(It's an angry look.)

The monsters actually *applaud*! "Thank you, Ghazt!" one calls out.

"We are in your debt, Grand Protector!" another cries.

Evie continues her parade of lie-filled pronouncements. "As Ghazt's second-in-command, I *promise* there will be NO MORE attacks! Never again will you face such terror!"

"She has zero control over whether Thrull attacks us again," I say to my friends. "She can't promise that!"

Dirk says, "She just did."

"Why isn't she even *mentioning* Thrull?" Quint asks, stunned. "If these monsters know that the mall's being targeted by the most vile villain in the land, some might leave and seek safety elsewhere. Some might stay and fight. But they have to know first! I *told* Ghazt about Thrull, but he and Evie are ignoring the most basic facts of what is happening here. *Why?*"

"Well," I say, thinking aloud, "because Evie and Ghazt have promised these monsters protection. But if the monsters realize that they *aren't* actually protected—"

"Then they'd have zero reason to put up with all their dumb rules and laws," June says, finishing my sentence. "And if *that* happens—"

"Evie and Ghazt lose their power," Quint says. "Power that grants them first dibs on everything that comes on board. Which not only gives them all the coolest items, but is also how they're finding information on where the Tower is."

"And," Dirk adds, "they'd lose their dibs on Drooler."

We're all silent for a moment, thinking about what that would mean for Drooler. For Dirk. For us. And for the monsters aboard the Mallusk.

"So in summation," Quint says "as long as Evie and Ghazt keep these monsters in the dark about the danger of Thrull, they'll continue to rule over the mall. Meaning they get to keep Drooler, and any day they may pick up some monster who tells them where the Tower is."

We watch the monsters, who are still nodding and sighing with relief at Evie's reassurances.

"Look," June says, "we knew it'd take more than just us to defeat Thrull. Trouble is, the residents of Mallusk City don't seem to care. It's like they think they're invincible as long as they're on here. But they're *not*. They're all in grave danger—unless they fight back. And they never *will* fight back, as long as Evie and Ghazt are in charge and keep feeding them these lies."

Glancing around, June spots a neon pink mall kiosk: Rockin' Ruby's Rockin' Karaoke Shoppe. She grabs one of the magenta microphones, spins the volume knob, and a screech erupts . . .

Hey, Evie! How do you know there won't be any more attacks? You got a crystal ball?

Before Evie can even respond, Smud appears by her side and reveals a Magic 8-Ball, still in the box. I'm pretty sure I see a Spencer's Gifts price tag on it.

"In fact I do!" Evie says, removing the Magic 8-Ball and giving it a good shake. "And it says: All signs point to . . . GHAZT KEEPING THE CITIZENS OF MALLUSK CITY SAFE!"

The monsters gasp in wonder at this magic.

"Oh, c'mon," I grumble. "That's not even a Magic 8-Ball answer. Magic 8-Balls only say like two things and neither of those things are about Ghazt."

The monsters cheer. She's telling them everything they want to hear.

But what they *need* to hear is the truth, even if they're not going to like it.

June scoops up the chunk of Howler necklace and shows it to the monsters. "This attack wasn't random. It happened because Thrull has taken an interest in the Mallusk. And we *all* need to deal with that! Because Thrull serves Ŗeżżőch and wants to bring Ŗeżżőch here to destroy EVERYTHING!"

The monsters murmur and shift. They look to Evie and Ghazt, waiting to be reassured. But June continues. "There are good monsters who want to stop Thrull. An alliance! And if you join us, together we *can* defeat Thrull and prevent Ŗeżżőch from coming!"

But the monsters are unconvinced . . .

"SEE?" Evie calls. "Jack, June—no one wants to hear all your doom and gloom. No one wants to sign up for your little war."

I glance at Dirk, who looks like he just got sucker punched. He's scared—*really* scared. Less than twenty-four hours ago, Dirk made a promise . . .

I have no idea if you can understand me, but here's the deal, Drooler.

You can help us defeat a very evil monster. And if you come with us, then I **promise** I will look out for you.

I will protect you, no matter what.

For a second, I forget about all the dimension-hanging-in-the-balance stuff. All I see is the absolute stomach-churning desperation on Dirk's face. We need to make sure Dirk keeps his promise to Drooler. Because if Dirk breaks that promise, it just might break *him*—break him into pieces just like one of Evie and Ghazt's Loot Globes . . .

And that's it. Of course!

"HEY, MONSTERS!" I shout, getting their attention. "I'VE GOT SOMETHING TO SAY!"

I pull the Slicer from behind my back, twirling it nonchalantly as I address the crowd. I know I can't use it to control zombies—not here, with Ghazt watching. But that doesn't mean it's powerless.

"You might think that what's happening beyond these walls has nothing to do with you . . . and hey, maybe you're right. What do I know? I'm just an orphan kid from a little place called Anytown . . ."

Out of the corner of my eye, I see June and Quint exchange a confused look. "Anytown?"

I grin and take a step toward one of the columns holding the monorail track. "I don't know everything," I say. "However . . ."

CRACK!

I swing the Slicer into the column with wannabe Babe Ruth strength. The column vibrates all the way up to the Food Court, to the monorail track, to the monorail. The car shifts and I jump back as—

SMASH!

A pallet of Evie and Ghazt's private loot falls, spilling incredible items across the floor.

"There is one thing I know for sure . . ."

The monsters gasp. Thrull building a Tower that will bring Ṛeżżőch to Earth and decimate our dimension? Not a problem for these guys. But the realization that they personally are being denied good loot? That's unacceptable!

"Hey! That's not true!" Evie screams. Her voice cracks. "That awesome stuff was gonna go out to everyone. It just got, um, misplaced. Misfiled. It's, uh—Smud's fault!"

Smud clearly hasn't been following the conversation. He's just happy to hear his name. He clasps his hands together and shakes them over his head, thinking he did something good. He is promptly pelted with a stale Cinnabon.

June looks my way and winks. I don't know what that wink means, and suddenly, I'm nervous . . .

June says, "Jack's right. You two are up there in your cozy tower, deciding who gets what. Sure, you claim to provide protection—but this mall needs someone who offers more than that. That's why . . . we challenge Ghazt TO AN ELECTION."

Everyone gasps.

"But not for the position of Grand Protector," June says. "It is the duly elected position of . . ."

"CLASS PRESIDENT!" I jump in. I flash June a grin. Nailed it, huh?

June closes her eyes briefly. "Nope. Close, but nope. MAYOR!"

She grabs my wrist, hops up on the pile of loot, and—

"Excuse me?" Evie squeaks.

"That's right!" June shouts. "MALL RESIDENTS, WE'RE HAVING AN ELECTION! THERE WILL BE A VOTE IN FIVE DAYS' TIME!"

"No!" Evie shouts "No, no, no! Um . . . Uh . . . NEW LAW! Yeah, Grand Protector Law #413, just announced: NO ELECTIONS. NO MAYORS."

But Evie's words are drowned out by monsters roaring with excitement.

"Sorry, Evie," June says, shrugging. "But the monsters seem to like the idea. Can't take it back now."

Evie just stands there, steaming.

"Catch you on the campaign trail!" June calls to Evie, then spins smartly and strides away.

I quickly catch up to June.

"Uh, hey, buddy? Wanna tell me what's going on?"

June smiles confidently. "You're running for mayor, that's what's going on," she says. "If you win, then we rescue Drooler, keep Evie and Ghazt from finding the Tower, and give these monsters a fair chance against Thrull."

"And if we lose?" I ask.

"Jack," she says, "I don't lose."

I like that "don't lose" strategy—it sounds like a winner. And it gets me excited.

I start to imagine myself as mayor. And you know what? I kinda dig it . . .

chapter ten

My mayoral campaign is off to a strong start—
we get our first supporter not fifteen minutes
later while walking down one of the mall's many
hallways in search of election supplies.

"You have my vote, Dirk's friend," says a low,
unfamiliar voice.

I pause and look around. Who on the Mallusk
knows Dirk? The voice is coming from a mall
kiosk: "Every Little Thing We Sell Is MAGIK."

The two unlikely friends catch up while I remember what Dirk told us about Yursl: weird conjurer type, helped him out in a pinch.

Here in her mall kiosk, she's surrounded by a cloud of glowing mist, and her skin glows a faint neon purple. It would all be very mystical if she weren't spinning a basketball on her fingertips and arguing with Dirk about best and worst Dunk Contest champions.

Also, the mist is not magical at all. I only figure that out after Yursl begins coughing, curses the fog machine at her feet, and shuts it off with a swift kick.

"I have so many questions . . ." Quint says, eyeing the kiosk with awe.

"Hey dudes," June says. "I'm going to check out that paper goods store. We're going to need a *lot* of paper goods for our campaign."

"Sure," I agree. "Wait, why?"

"Jack." June raises her eyebrows at me. "Trust the expert."

"I'll help," Dirk offers. "I'll do whatever it takes. I have a lot riding on you winning," he adds. "Y'know?"

I nod, picturing Drooler in his cage. "I know."

Dirk gives a wave. "Yursl, I'll see you around?"

"Not if I see you first," she says. Then, after

a moment, she adds, "Which I will. Of course.
'Cause, y'know. *Conjurer powers.*"

With Dirk gone, Quint can ask this strange
witch-type lady all his questions. Which,
because it's Quint, are a *lot* of questions.

"Do you think . . ." Quint seems suddenly bashful. "Could I maybe learn how to use some of these conjurer objects? Would you possibly . . . teach me?"

But I can't wait for Yursl to answer, because I'm realizing I maybe made a giganto mistake.

"Uh, hey, guys? Er . . . ma'am?" I say, lifting my hands, which I have just stuck inside one of those little finger traps. "Uh, there's something wrong with this finger—OW! It's, like, alive and—yep, it is currently gnawing on my pointer fingers. Could you remove this now, please, please?"

Yursl just stares at Quint, totally ignoring my finger-devouring dilemma. "Your stick . . . It reminds me of a conjurer's cane. May I hold it?"

Quint happily hands it over. "Conjurer's cane . . ." he says softly, and I can tell he likes the sound of that—way more than "staff" or "stick."

"Yes, very reminiscent . . ." Yursl says, turning it over in her hands. "The shape, of course. But more than that . . . its *intention*."

"Um . . . 'intention'?" Quint asks. "Well, when I began building it, I had extensive plans . . . but then we got started on this road trip, and I haven't had much time to work on it."

I MEAN ITS PURPOSE—

OK, we get it! You're very wowed by Quint's stick-cane and its INTENTION and PURPOSE.

Now, please . . . GET THESE FINGER EATERS OFF MY FINGERS!

"Oh . . . Oh!" Quint says, finally noticing that I'm in real danger. "Right. Um, Ms. Yursl? Would you mind helping out my friend?"

"Let me put that question back to you," Yursl responds. "Since you're interested in conjurer objects, what would *you* use to free your friend's hands from the grasp of the Schloop?"

"Hmm . . ." Quint taps his chin as he looks around the kiosk, his eyes sliding across bubbling cauldrons, oddly shaped bottles, and glowing keys. "There are just so many options . . . and I don't know what most of them do . . ."

"Quint!" I holler. "Just choose one, OK?"

Quint's gaze lands back on the basketball that Yursl was spinning when we first walked in here. "That," he says.

"Dude," I say, "you can pick from magical crystals and wands and you choose a *basketball*? Do you *want* my fingers to get chewed off?"

But Yursl just smiles. She picks the basketball back up, places it in front of the Schloop on my fingers, and sets the basketball spinning again.

Instantly, the Schloop begins to purr—then its grip relaxes fully. I breathe a sigh of relief and return the Schloop to the shelf, blowing on my fingers to bring life back into them.

"Whoa," Quint breathes, staring at Yursl in wonder. "You used the spinning basketball to hypnotize it!"

"And *you*, Quint," Yursl replies, "passed the test! You proved yourself worthy. I shall grant your request for teaching. You shall be my . . ."

"Apprentice?" Quint jumps in. "Am I going to be a conjurer's apprentice?"

"*Intern*," Yursl says. "You shall be my intern. Thoroughly unpaid. This isn't a fairy tale."

"Intern . . ." Quint says, clearly loving the sound of the word.

"I will allow you to try on the Conjurer's Cloak," Yursl says, tossing it to Quint. "Just once."

Quint's trembling with excitement as he swirls the cloak over his shoulder. And he *does* look pretty legit in it . . .

Quint's smile is electric. I realize then that I haven't seen Quint this purely happy in a long time. This is his *thing*.

So I decide to make myself scarce; let Quint and Yursl bond over their nerdy-cool science/conjuring stuff.

And as I walk away, I hear—

"HEY! SULLIVAN! You're a candidate now—walk like one!"

I spin around. It's June, cruising up to me on one of those mall security guard Segways. She's towing a Radio Flyer wagon loaded up with tons of campaign supplies.

"Shoulders back. Head high," June says, immediately in campaign manager mode. "You gotta look electable. Stately. Commanding."

I hop on the Radio Flyer and give her my most leadership-y pose . . .

"Eh, you kinda look like a dog in need of a fire hydrant. But we'll work on it! Hey, ready to see our campaign headquarters?" June asks. "Johnny Steve picked out a spot."

I follow her through crowded, bustling corridors until we reach . . .

"Better than good!" I say. "And thanks for keeping an eye on my zombies."

I swing the Slicer toward a pop-up camping tent. "Take a load off, dudes," I say, and Alfred, Lefty, and Glurm shuffle off to get comfy.

I grab a sweatshirt to use as a pillow, then take a running leap for a trampoline, and about seven seconds after my butt bounces off the springs, I'm ready to sleep.

My friends come back soon after. Quint, still glowing, goes straight for a hammock while Dirk snuggles up in an inflatable pool. June, however, is still hyped up and working.

"Get some rest!" June shouts. "The campaign starts tomorrow . . ."

The campaign. Our best shot at freeing Drooler, getting these monsters to stand up and hear the truth, and finding a way off the Mallusk.

And then, maybe, I can tell my buddies what's going on with my hand . . .

I look at the Cosmic Hand again.

It looks thicker.

And that's scary. Too scary to think about. I shove it underneath my sweatshirt pillow, and soon my eyelids are shutting . . .

chapter eleven

Dirk wakes me up. Apparently, he's taking full advantage of our new home—he's dressed head to toe in neon workout gear. He hands me a brand-new ultra-hydration water bottle filled with cherry Pepsi. "You're gonna need it," he says. "June is ready and rarin'."

He's not kidding. I'm still wiping gunk from my eyes, and June has already started in . . .

Campaign Strategy

Welcome to the war room, boys. Here's the deal. We have four days until the election. If you all do what I say, Jack Sullivan WILL be elected Mayor of Mallusk City.

JACK
R
YOR

JACK
JACK
4
MALLUSK
CITY
MA OR R

June says, "First, the bad news. Ghazt and Evie will be tough to beat, because they *have* kept the monsters safe."

"But they were *already* safe," Quint says. "The Mallusk was not constantly under attack. Johnny Steve said as much."

"Sure," June says. "But Evie and Ghazt are taking credit for keeping them safe . . . and it's working."

"What about the loot thing I did, though? That probably helped, right?" I say. "Validation, please?" I add with a pleading smile.

"Now that pleading smile, Jack, *that's* the look of a politician!" June says. "And yes, your loot thing was good. However, Evie and Ghazt are now giving out TONS OF GOOD LOOT. Evie was up at dawn, hurling 'gifts' at the residents."

"Guess who's now the proud owner of *nine* shoes?" Johnny Steve brags.

"But there is good news," June continues. "The monsters think that Evie and Ghazt are pretty darn annoying. The biggest complaint is Evie and Ghazt's endless new laws."

"Evie likes being in charge. The power," I say. "That's her whole deal."

June nods. "The laws are supposed to be fun.

But I think they both may be unclear on the actual definition of 'fun.'"

"Oh yes," Johnny Steve chimes in. "Wacky Hat Wednesday has been a consistent failure . . ."

You call that propeller beanie wacky? It's not! It's whimsical at best! I hope that propeller works!

"So it's like a toss-up?" I ask. "Right now, either of us could win?"

"Nope!" Johnny Steve says. "Definitely you're losing."

June slams her fist on the table—and it promptly shatters in two. "Oops, forgot about Blasty," she says. "Ahem. That was just supposed to be an inspiring and leadership-y desk pound—not a property-damaging one."

"I thought it was cool," Dirk says with a shrug.

June says, "We can overcome the monsters' early opinions. Because right here, we've got . . . the dream team!"

"WE DO?" Johnny Steve exclaims giddily. "Oh, I am so excited to meet Charles Barkley. The greatest of all human golfers!"

Dirk shakes his head. "Not that dream team, Johnny Steve. She just means . . . y'know . . . us."

June leans forward. "And especially you, Jack. The candidate . . ."

"And I am . . ." June says, tapping her badge, "THE CAMPAIGN MANAGER. I ran my first campaign in fourth grade—and *won*. I single-handedly got Martha Heyward elected student body president, despite her endless verbal gaffes *and* her insistence on delivering all speeches via her creepy ventriloquist dummy, Sir Woody . . ."

Pizza for lunch every Friday!

That's already a thing, Martha! It's called Pizza Lunch Friday and it literally happens every Friday!

"Wow," I say. "If you got *her* elected, just imagine what you can do with a candidate who *doesn't* make verbal giraffes!"

"Giraffes," Dirk chuckles. "Love giraffes. Nothing beats a talking giraffe."

129

"FOCUS, BOYS!" June says. Her eyes are beady and sugar-charged. "First, we need a campaign slogan. Something catchy. Memorable, but not cheesy. Let's do some brainstorming here. Total blue sky. No such thing as a bad idea. Just throw 'em on the board."

June has made a makeshift cork wall out of a dozen dart boards, and we pin up some ideas. She says we need to *visualize* the slogan.

Quint hasn't offered any slogan suggestions, so I shoot him a glance. But he doesn't notice; he's affixing a small knob to his conjurer's cane. I realize he's been fiddling with it this entire time. And that's just fine with me—feels like interdimensional conjurer stuff is more valuable in the fight against ultimate evil than campaign slogans anyway.

"Y'know . . ." June says after staring at our ideas for a long while. "I'll just think about these later. By myself. Alone."

"Sure!" I say. "Love the dedication, June—really good stuff."

"The good news," June says, like she's reassuring herself as much as me, "is that they don't have a platform. *We* do."

"And it's a good one!" Dirk says. "Solid brass! Got it at the Platform Hut."

June shakes her head. "No. I'm talking about giving the monsters the *truth*. That Thrull is a danger that must be faced—*together*."

She reveals a big mall directory and says, "We need to canvas each of the mall's neighborhoods, getting the Jack Sullivan promise out to every citizen of Mallusk City."

I leap to my feet. "And I know just the place to start . . ."

After an hour of waving at monsters, handing out buttons, and eating free barbecue, I'm brimming with confidence.

"Quint, this 'running for mayor' thing is a breeze. I think I've got this in the bag—"

VROOOM!

Quint spins. "Our BoomKarts!"

"Speeding past us!" I cry. "Driven by our enemies! That's just twisting the knife."

My face falls.

We follow the sound of the BoomKarts—*our* BoomKarts—to a massive indoor ski jump. Huge tall monsters are using round, flat monsters like sleds, shooting downhill then launching off an epic jump. Everyone seems to be having the time of their lives.

At the top of the slope, Smud hands out Ghazt-shaped popsicles. At least, I hope they're Ghazt-shaped popsicles and not frozen rats.

Ghazt lounges beneath the jump, relaxing in the biggest blow-up pool I've ever seen.

My plan is to confidently stomp toward Ghazt, my sworn enemy and current opponent. But instead, I end up slipping and sliding across the ice-topped snow, finally tumbling to the frozen floor. I look less than electable.

"Very smooth, Jack," Evie says, stomping over in a pair of heavy-duty snow boots.

"What happened to that bit yesterday where we were gonna fight?" I mutter. "'Cause I still feel like fighting them. Also, my butt is cold."

"It's far more dignified to beat you at the ballot box," Evie says.

Quint, who's using his cane as a sort of ski-pole, easily strides over. "Fancy sled-jump parties and rat popsicles do *not* a campaign make," he says. "Come on, Jack. We'll show Evie what a *real* candidate looks like."

"You bet we will," I say as I start to stand. But I slip. Again. And I fall. Again. I try three more times before I finally just give up and crawl my way toward the exit.

"Very silly!" Evie calls after us. "Apparently, a real candidate looks *very silly!*"

The monsters must agree, because they're howling with laughter by the time I finally reach the door.

So yeah, that could have gone better. But Quint and I remain upbeat! We press on with the whirlwind, whistle-stop campaign tour. Next up: the depths of the Mallusk, in hopes of securing the Junker vote. But to get the Junkers to even consider voting for me, they want me to prove I can hang with them.

And by "hang with them"—they mean *hang
on*. Thankfully, the Cosmic Hand's suckers are
a big help . . .

Next stop: the mall's food scene. These
monsters are *really* into eating—and word is Chef
Rotbrood's legendary Blood-Eyed Blaze sandwich
is the mall's *must-eat* meal.

"Listen up, Jack," Quint whispers as we enter
a converted Johnny Rockets. "If you finish one of
Chef Rotbrood's sandwiches, you'll win the vote
of *all* of the mall's foodies."

Chef Rotbrood is waiting at a booth in the back. But as soon I sit down, I learn there's a catch. A big one . . .

Fifty-seven minutes in, I take my final bite. The plate is empty—and everyone's cheering . . . even ol' Rotbrood.

"Quint . . ." I manage as I shuffle out of the restaurant. "I need a nap."

Quint slaps me on the back. "Soon! Only nineteen more campaign stops to go!"

From there, we play cards with a squad of monster wrestlers, high-five every Flipapik in the monster circus, and even practice lines with a traveling monster theater company.

At the giant monstrous spinal cord in the mall's hub, I think I even win over the Barterers and Traders Union . . .

We're heading back to Hey Sport, ready to call it a night, when I hear monsters whispering my name. And then laughing! I realize they're all watching one of the mall's big-screen displays.

I look up at the screen—and I see *me*! Slipping on the ice earlier that day. The whole mall is watching me flop about like a fool!

DO YOU REALLY WANT A MAYOR WHO SLIPS UP AGAIN AND AGAIN AND AGAIN?

BONK

KRAK

VOTE GHAZT FOR MALL MAYOR

"A smear ad!" Quint gasps.

And there's no question who's behind it: Evie and Ghazt. They're proudly watching the screen.

My campaign is going south—and fast.

Thankfully, June shows up to bail me out. "Evie, Ghazt, honorable monsters," she calls out. "We all know being good at walking on slippery ice isn't what this election is really about. What do you say we settle this like *serious candidates*?"

YES! I WILL SPILL THE BLOOD OF ALL!

What he meant to say was, "I will spill my blood for all of you!" That's how much he cares!

June shoots me a look, almost like an apology for what she's about to propose. "It's time we heard from you, the citizens. Heard your questions and answered your concerns! TOWN HALL! TOMORROW!"

Evie frowns, suddenly looking less confident. I'm guessing Ghazt's not great in a Q&A situation. I heard a few of his speeches today, and they're *terrifying*. There's always lots of talk about crushing unworthy parasites beneath demonic bootheels.

But Evie quickly drops the frown, projecting confidence. "You're on! Tomorrow! Three p.m."

"We'll be there early!" June says.

"We'll be there earlier!" Evie shoots back.

"Then we'll be there *late*. So you look like you had the time wrong!"

"But we already set a time and everyone knows it," Evie says. "So that won't work!"

"Then we'll tell them it's daylight saving time and their big grand protector forgot to warn them about the impending clock roll-back, failing to protect them from the embarrassment of being super late to a rad event!"

"No more!" Evie barks. "It is settled . . . Three p.m., tomorrow. And my watch says your time is almost up."

June squints at Evie's wrist. "Your watch says Timex."

"YES I KNOW THAT! But do you hear the clock-ticking sound? TICK. TICK. TICK. That is the sound of your time being *almost up*."

June frowns. "I don't hear anything. That's a digital watch. They don't make ticking sounds."

That's when Quint, thankfully, pulls June away. "THREE P.M. ON THE DOT. SEE YA THEN!"

This is all happening so fast, and nobody is asking the candidate whether *I* want a town hall! It's one thing to shake some hands/feet/general monstrous digits, kiss some monster babies, and eat big sandwiches.

But a town hall? That's, like, *debating*. And debating is pretty much just organized arguing. And every time I've argued with a pure-evil monster, I've settled that argument with the Slicer. Not words!

I didn't sign up for this.

But then I look at June and Dirk. June looks so excited and determined. She believes in me.

And Dirk looks so desperate. He *needs* me to win. For him. For Drooler.

I can't let them down.

chapter twelve

The next morning, I sit up on my trampoline bed.
And I notice it's quiet.

I hop-step-shuffle into a pair of jogging pants
and hurry across the store to our campaign
headquarters.

No June, no Dirk, no Quint. Oh man, if I
overslept for the definitely-happening-at-three-
p.m. town hall, I'm in trouble.

The only ones around are my zombies,
lounging in a pop-up camping tent. I've fully
outfitted them with mall-made weapons: a patio
umbrella for Alfred, a rain stick from some
organic crystals store for Lefty, and a heavy
motorized pogo stick for Glurm. They can't
attack without my command, but they can still
look intimidating.

"Hey, guys," I say. "Where is everyone?"

I only get moans. Don't know what else I
expected. But I ask again, waving my Slicer this
time. In response, Alfred holds up a Post-it note
that says "Gone to staff meeting."

"Staff meeting?" I say aloud. "I don't remember June scheduling a staff meeting. And where else would it be but here?"

I throw on a June-approved mayoral candidate hoodie and head off in search of my friends. I'm passing by Every Little Thing We Sell Is MAGIK when—

Ohhhh. Staff meeting, I think. *Right.*

Quint's eyes light up when he notices me. "Jack!" he says, waving his staff. "Come look!"

"Whoa," I say. "What have you done to that thing? It looks like a cyborg shower curtain."

The conjurer's cane has been given the full Quint treatment—loaded up with gadgets, thingamajigs, and doodads. But Yursl must have made some modifications, too, because a tiny Nerf basketball now hangs from a net on the side of the cane.

Quint flicks a switch, and the foam ball begins to glow, bathing Quint's face in swirling color. Smiling, Quint jumps into an explanation of the conjurer's cane's upgraded features.

Pop-out antenna

Battery

B-ball sling-net

"If you flick this tiny joystick," Quint explains, "it can recognize radio frequencies within a one-hundred-mile radius!"

"It is a most unusual form of conjuring . . ." Yursl croaks mysteriously.

"Well, yeah," Quint says. "I suppose science *is* a bit like conjuring, in a way."

"A *new* sort of conjuring," she says. "We must tread lightly. The wrong mixture of science and spell, and . . . who knows? Your entire molecular structure could be displaced—transported to another location!"

Quint shrugs that off like it's nothing, but I can tell his science-brain is flipping out right now.

I have a few hours until the town hall, and just one full day remaining until the election. So I throw everything out the window for the afternoon and just try to have *fun* with it . . .

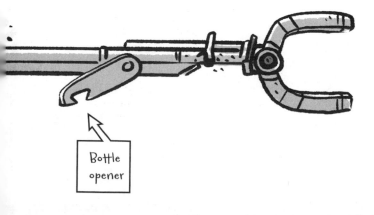

Bottle opener

GOOD TIMES CAMPAIGNING ON THE MALLUSK MONTAGE!

I show up to the town hall right on time and give myself a well-deserved high five.

There are thousands of monsters gathered at the Play Area & Rendezvous Plaza. June is waiting, holding out a fresh outfit.

Quick, duder, time to get spiffy. This is your town hall outfit: blue suit, three-peak pocket square, tie with just the right amount of stripe thickness, and this awesome mall pin.

Jack, bro . . . what have you gotten yourself into?

I sigh. I just wanna curl up under a very heavy blanket and read comics for about twenty-seven hours. The end of the world is wearing me down.

"June," I say. "There is *no way* I'm wearing that. They're gonna think I'm a big dork!"

"You are a big dork."

"Yeah, but I don't need to advertise it!"

Before June can protest further, I march toward the stage. I've got an awful feeling in my gut—like I was just called to the front of the class to do a book report on a book I forgot to read.

I'm very aware of the hundreds of monsters staring up at me. I glance around—looking for something to casually-cool lean on. No luck. Maybe I should hook one thumb in my belt loop, and sort of flap my hand? That's cool, right?

Suddenly, booming music erupts from all around us! I spot Evie near the stage, cranking a stereo dial. The song is "Hit the Road, Jack"—and it is blasting. The monsters go wild, shouting, hollering, and singing along!

"Ugh," I groan. "*And* they know the lyrics!"

And then—

Aww man, he's wearing the outfit! Lesson learned: listen to June.

A knot twists in my stomach, and my heart is about halfway up my throat. Any progress I made this morning feels lost—and the town hall hasn't even started yet!

Johnny Steve waddles up on stage. "Settle, citizens, settle. I know you're excited. We've all been looking forward to this for a long time. Nearly one full day."

My head is spinning. This is too much. It's like running for sixth-grade class president, except the duties aren't just school-store budgeting and packing the yearbook full of flattering photos of yourself—the duties are *defeating evil and leading innocent monsters to survival.*

"The candidates will now introduce themselves," Johnny Steve says.

"GHAZT GOES FIRST!" Smud shouts from the audience. "'Cause he's my boss!"

June shoots me a look, like, *More*.

"Oh, and I'm running for class president," I mumble. "I mean . . . mayor."

"And now," Johnny Steve says, "the candidates will take your questions."

But Johnny Steve fails to say "one at a time" and the monsters erupt, showering us with a barrage of questions . . .

"DOES HEALTHY HAVE TO MEAN IT TASTES BAD?"

"IF GHAZT IS SO GREAT, WHY DOESN'T HE HAVE MORE FRIENDS?"

"IS THIS A BUNION OR A SORE?"

"IS SMUD AS FUNNY AS HE IS CUTE?"

"WHY DOES THIS DIMENSION SMELL LIKE HAMBURGERS?"

"IF YOU CAN STOP THE HOWLERS, CAN YOU ALSO STOP THE HORRIBLE NIGHTMARES THAT CAUSE ME TO HOWL IN MY SLEEP?"

"BLACK LICORICE OR RED?!"

This is all too disorganized and unruly for Evie. A few monsters snicker as she suddenly charges to the front of the stage—

We held this town hall because we **thought** you were responsible enough to handle it. But right now, you're not acting like responsible citizens.

That just makes the monsters laugh harder.

"I'LL WAIT," she says. "I've got all day . . ."

Another round of giggling.

"Your actions here today are an embarrassment to this mall."

A ton more giggling.

Ghazt snaps. "I WILL DEVOUR THE SOUL OF THE NEXT CREATURE WHO DARES UTTER EVEN A CHUCKLE! YOU WILL SUFFER ETERNAL TORMENT!"

"OK then, actually, we're gonna wrap this up!" Evie says, eyeing Ghazt nervously. "Final question! And I will call on . . . Smud."

"Hey!" Quint shouts. "The question-asking person cannot be affiliated with the candidate!"

Smud stands up. He's reading from a card. "This question is for each of you. What—if any—experience do you have as a general, warlord, or Cosmic Entity? And why should that experience give us confidence in your ability to lead us?"

OK, *what*? This is super bogus.

Even though Smud is asking an obviously planted question, Ghazt still looks like he wants to leap down and tear his henchmonster apart—just because this is all so beneath him.

Ghazt roars, "What experience, you ask?"

The audience doesn't like that answer. They
must not buy that I'm a dude who bathes in tears.
Ghazt thinks he's got me on the ropes, because
he jumps back in . . .

"The small human boy is nothing. I am A GENERAL. WITH POWERS. I can control the undead humans! I can control an *army*!"

This gets the monster crowd even more excited. My chest starts heaving. Ghazt's lying to their faces. He no longer possesses the power to control zombies, but the monsters are eating up the lies.

Ghazt continues, "And THAT is why I alone can keep you safe. If needed, I can control an entire army of undead humans to protect the Mallusk! I can make the undead humans do *anything* I please!"

The crowd erupts with more excited gasps and whispers. "Show us!" one monster shouts. And then others join in, chanting, "SHOW US! SHOW US! SHOW US!"

"Well, I would," Ghazt says. Then, sounding very disappointed, he adds, "Except there are no undead humans here for me to control."

I think about my Slicer. I could do it. I *can* do it.

I can summon Alfred, Lefty, and Glurm right here and now—and show everyone who *really* has the power to control the undead.

The moment is *too big to ignore.*

The pulsing pull of the Cosmic Hand is *too much to resist.*

So I reach behind my back.

My eyes close as my fingers wrap around the blade. The Cosmic Hand vibrates and tingles. I feel a flash—like someone, somewhere, is watching me. It's not totally unlike how I felt when I grabbed hold of Blargus's vines and *jacked in*. When I saw Thrull and he saw me.

Suddenly—

GRRR-BUUUMP!
BRRR-BRRRUMMM

Everything jerks and jolts. My eyes fly open. The Mallusk rocks and rolls and everyone lurches forward.

"The Mallusk is stopping!" one monster exclaims.

"Woo-hoo! Excursion!" another monster shouts.

The monsters all race for the doors. It's like they all just found out they were going on a surprise field trip.

Apparently, the town hall has officially ended, and that's just fine with me.

June, Quint, Dirk, and I follow the monsters. Out in the corridors, we see them eagerly grabbing things to barter and trade.

We head up to the top level, outside, to the Adventure Mini-Golf Driving Range near the bow of the Mallusk.

"Whoa . . ." Quint says.

The view is stunningly expansive . . . .

chapter thirteen

The mall's huge main entrance opens, and my buddies and I are among the first to exit. The sun is blindingly bright, ricocheting off yellow desert earth.

We disembark down the Mallusk's huge, single gangplank. Since shopping malls don't typically have, y'know, *gangplanks*—this is a wide, cobbled-together thing built from splintered mall flooring, rusted metal pried off cars, and other scavenged items. Thankfully, there are railings—red ropes taken from the movie theater—and I grip them tight.

When we finally step onto the hot desert ground, I'm surprised by how *solid* it feels. I had gotten used to the Mallusk's constant movement.

I take in the scene. An interstate road, running parallel to the Mallusk, stretches both directions into the distance. Along the road are overturned cars, a few flipped RVs, and a rest stop. Ahead of us are more abandoned vehicles, some small buildings, and—

"WHOA!" I exclaim. "Huge monster! Dead ahead!"

"Relax," Dirk says. "Huge *stucco* monster."

"Another of those big giant dinosaurs," Quint says. "Like the one Alfred, Lefty, and Glurm posed in during the road trip."

"I don't know who decided to scatter big fake dinosaurs all across the country," I say, relaxing. "But I like the way they think."

Suddenly, two little monsters appear in the mouth of the dinosaur, waving happily.

These two little monsters must have been *very eagerly* awaiting the arrival of someone to trade with, because they move with incredible quickness.

A folding table is hurled from the dinosaur's mouth, followed by a big suitcase. Then a long rope, made from what looks like monster hair, is unfurled, and the two monsters descend.

"A pair of post-apocalyptic Rapunzels," June says. "Rad."

In a flash, the table is unfolded, the suitcase is unpacked, and items are on display. "Gaze upon our wares!" one monster shouts.

"All prices negotiable!" the other quickly adds.

"It's a little monster yard sale," Dirk says. "Cute."

We're jostled aside as dozens of monsters hurry off the gangplank, rushing toward the table. Johnny Steve is among them, using his walking sword to navigate the rocky ground.

But as we get close, I realize that a monster yard sale—which sounds like the most amazing thing *ever*—is actually kinda dull. I take a quick peek at the objects for sale: an old microwave, some dinged-up silverware, and piles of musty old books.

I'm less interested in this lousy little roadside sale—and more interested in *why* the Mallusk stopped. Why now? Why here? I can't imagine it stopped because it wanted to buy a busted toaster.

"Let's find out what the Mallusk is up to," I say, and the four of us hike toward the front end of the great creature. Walking its length, I notice the many scars and scrapes and wounds that mark her rough skin.

Far ahead, I see a wide river running perpendicular to the Mallusk's path. A bridge, dotted with abandoned cars, crosses the river. As we near the front, the Mallusk lets out a sudden, earth-trembling WAIL! And then—

SMASH!

The bridge is instantly demolished as the Mallusk slams her head downward, through the bridge, plunging her face-parts into the river water below.

Ice-cold water splashes us as the Mallusk pushes her head deeper into the water.

For a split second, I think I hear the shriek of a Howler. But the sound is weak, muted—and I realize it must be something else.

More traders, maybe? About to come over the rubble in the distance?

I glance back at the little garage sale. The two monsters are hastily packing up. They leave quicker than they arrived—in a flash, the table is folded up, the suitcase is in hand, and they're speedily hoisting themselves back up into the mouth of the dinosaur.

That can't be good, I think. *What do they know that we don't?*

Then I hear the sound again—something like a huge creature scuttling. The noise comes from just beyond the rest stop.

A fluttery feeling fills my stomach. "Guys, I think we might want to get back on board the—"

BOOM!

A pocket of nearby earth erupts, instantly filling the air with clouds of dirt and dust. It's so thick that, for a moment, I can't see more than a few feet in front of me. Screams erupt behind us—but I can't see that far.

"That was a *bomb*!" June shouts, staggering back. We all huddle together, spinning, searching.

"Don't see any flying monsters dropping bombs," Dirk says, looking to the sky. "So where'd it come from?"

Then I see it.

A monstrosity climbing up and over the rest stop. The building cracks and sags under the monster's weight.

I realize I've seen this monster before—or one like it. A cousin or something. The Shovel Scorpion: we encountered it weeks earlier, during our road trip stop at the World's Largest Collection of the World's Smallest Stuff . . .

But this monster, here, now—this is like a leveled-up version. Like the same general species, but boss status.

Terrified screams from inhuman lungs fill the air. I glance back—some Mallusk monsters are hurrying back to the gangplank. Others take cover, ducking behind pickup trucks and scurrying beneath picnic tables. A few look paralyzed by uncertainty—they do nothing, because they're afraid whatever move they make next might be the wrong one.

A shadow blocks the sun for a split second—then another explosion!

This time, I realize why bombs are raining down on us, even though there are no monsters circling in the sky above.

"Look!" I shout. "The bombs are being fired from that fleshy launcher on the monster's back!"

"Like mortar shells," Dirk says.

The next explosion is close. An RV flips up into the air. Clouds of dirt and chunks of sandy ground erupt beneath it.

The smoke and debris clear—and I see the monster fully . . .

"It's got, like, a pilot!" Quint says, pointing. "But it's just a torso, attached to the monster's back! I've never seen anything like that before."

"And these aren't the type of bombs that just go BOOM," June says. "These are something totally different. Look . . ."

I glance at the flipped RV. Something beneath it is pushing the vehicle aside, lifting it off the ground. And what I see below, in the crater left by the bomb, turns my blood to ice . . .

chapter fourteen

A dozen skeletal arms and hands push the RV upward and then, finally, hurl it aside! Instantly, a swarm of bony figures crawls from out of the crater.

Nearby, I see scattered, disconnected bones. They rattle and shiver—then also begin to rise.

"Thrull's skeleton soldiers. . . " I gasp.

"It's the bombs!" Quint says. "Each one is a tightly wrapped sphere of bone and vine."

"And when the bomb blows," Dirk says, "the bones scatter."

"And the scattered bones join together, forming skeleton soldiers," June realizes.

"So . . . bone bombs, yeah?" I say. "Can we call them bone bombs?"

The vines seek out other vines. They snap out, lashing around bones, connecting them. They form skeletons. Skeletons that are now on the move . . .

Some rise fully formed; others are still piecing themselves together as they start toward us. They are malformed monstrosities, with legs where arms should be, skulls turned the wrong way, spinal cords trailing like nightmarish tails.

And just our luck—these malformed monstrosities still manage to wield weapons. One flashes a hatchet with a monster-scale blade. Another swings a bone club covered in spiky teeth.

"Oh, my word!" a voice cries out. It's Johnny Steve, ducked behind the base of the dinosaur. A few other monsters join him.

But that cover won't keep them safe for long.

More Mortar Monsters appear, all approaching the Mallusk. Bone bombs continue to explode, scattering bone and vine and forming new skeletons. All along the length of the Mallusk, the monstrosities are rising and marching.

"We've gotta get back inside!" June shouts.

"The enemy is blocking our only path," Quint says, pointing to the skeletons climbing over the RV.

"Then we go through them," June says.

Dirk smiles. "That's my kinda plan."

And with that, we charge forward, barreling into the monstrous mob! I swing the Slicer wildly, crack after crack ringing out as baseball bat meets bone. A long, swiping arm—protruding from the place where the skeleton's head should be—is severed.

But all around us, the bony figures roar—twisting and fusing and rising higher to engulf us in a chaotic, close-quarters brawl . . .

We're able to split the skeleton horde into two groups, allowing us to fight our way through the middle. I feel a sharp breeze as one final ax swing just misses me, then—

"See ya around!" June shouts as we push through, leaving them in the dust.

"But there's bad news ahead, friends," Quint says, pointing to the stucco dinosaur.

A skeleton pack has descended upon it, swarming Johnny Steve and a group of Mallusk City monsters. Johnny Steve slashes his walking sword at the skeletons, keeping them at bay. The monsters move back and forth along the dinosaur's tail, ducking beneath it as one skeleton attacks, then hopping back over it as more approach.

"Get them back to the Mallusk!" I shout at Johnny Steve. "Go now! You have a clear—"

BOOM!

The bone bomb explodes in the open space between the gangplank and the dinosaur.

The rising skeleton monstrosities have cut the only path back to the Mallusk. Terrified screams fill the air as our monster friends realize they're trapped . . .

The next bone bomb impacts against the Mallusk's hide.

She lifts her head out of the water and wails. Then her legs jam into the ground, shaking the earth.

"She's got the right idea," Quint says. "Leaving."

"But we can't let her leave without us," Dirk says. "And not without Johnny Steve and the other monsters, either."

I spot Evie, Ghazt, and Smud in the middle of a sea of monsters, already halfway up the gangplank, streaming for the safety of the Mallusk.

"Boy, all of Ghazt's stuff about being a 'protector' is right out the window now, huh?" June says.

And that's just fine with me.

Because if we're gonna get out of here—we need help. The four of us are overpowered— no way of rescuing the monsters trapped at the dinosaur. But with *seven* of us, we stand a chance. I need Alfred, Glurm, and Lefty.

I know that revealing my full powers—*Ghazt's full powers*, which are now inside my blade—

will be bad. When Evie and Ghazt know exactly what I can do, there will be no more discussion, no more bargaining. Plus, I remember—way too clearly—what Ghazt said about chomping off arms.

But calling my zombies is the only shot I have at ensuring the mall monsters' safety. Maybe I'll get lucky, and Ghazt won't see. Maybe not. It's a risk I have to take.

"Radical zombie trio!" I call out as I look up at the mall. "I need you guys!"

And I *swing* the Slicer.

Moments later, Alfred, Glurm, and Lefty appear at one of the mall's outdoor dining areas. "Come do radical zombie fighting!" I shout, and I swing the Slicer again. My Zombie Squad leaps over the side, then slide-bounces down the Mallusk's hide, all the way to the ground.

"FIGHT!" I cry, swinging again, and they charge into the fray at the bottom of the gangplank, wielding their mall-constructed weapons. Alfred uses his patio umbrella like a lance. Lefty's rain stick is now a battering ram. Glurm wields his pogo stick like a jackhammer.

The ground quakes again—the Mallusk gearing up to go. Nearly all of the monsters are safely back on board now, watching from windows, landings, and terraces.

But Johnny Steve and a dozen others aren't there yet.

"¥æżżőð ßüçå"

Oh no . . .

One Mortar Monster is close, climbing atop an overturned tractor trailer. The Pilot-Thing raises a hand, points to the gangplank, and gives an order: "¥æżżő̋ð ßüçå flğğdě".

I see the Mortar Monster's launcher bulge and expand, preparing to fire.

"Johnny Steve and the monsters aren't going to make it to the gangplank in time," June says.

"Alfred, Lefty, Glurm—swarm that overgrown Red Lobster reject!" I shout, giving the command as I swing the Slicer.

The zombies charge! They scramble up the trailer, then throw themselves atop the monster just as it fires—

PFHWOOMP!

The bomb launches wildly, sailing backward. My zombies are blasted off—but they quickly get to their feet, A-OK.

"We made it!" Johnny Steve shouts as he and the last of the mall monsters safely race up the gangplank.

The ground shakes again—dirt and concrete erupting. The Mallusk is beginning to move.

"We need to get back on board!" Dirk shouts.

"Alfred, Lefty, Glurm—up the side!" I
command. With a swish of the slicer, they're
back on the Mallusk, scrambling up her hide.

One final bone bomb explodes behind us—
jet-rocketing us forward as we race toward the
accelerating Mallusk. We leap, grabbing on
to the gangplank just as the bottom snaps off,
flipping across the ground.

OOOOOOOOOOOOOOOOOOM!

The Mallusk is moving fast, ripping across the terrain, plowing through roadside shopping centers. The Mortar Monsters continue launching bone bombs, but each falls short.

The Mallusk rocks and pitches like a sailboat over choppy waters. Wind whips over me as I look back—the Mortar Monsters are now just tiny shapes in the distance. In just minutes, the Mallusk has put miles between us and the enemy.

The gangplank is slowly being hoisted up and inside. We all grip the railing tight, carefully pulling ourselves up.

"Jack, if you win this election," Dirk grunts as he climbs, "first new rule: no unplanned pit stops."

Before I can respond, a voice says—

"*YOU.*"

We all freeze.

Ghazt appears at the mall's entryway. Evie stands beside him. Smud's in the rear, trying and failing to peer over Ghazt's massive frame. I take one look at their faces, and I know exactly what's happened.

Ghazt saw me use my powers.

His powers.

There is a sudden flash of fur and then Ghazt is leaping, mouth curled back, beastly yellow fangs snapping. I'm about to scream, I want to scream, but there's no time . . .

chapter fifteen

YOU HAVE MY POWERS!!

Ghazt sails over my friends and his paws punch me square in the chest. I tumble down the gangplank, hands scraping the metal grating, barely hanging on.

Ghazt stalks toward me.

"Would you believe me if I told you I don't know what you're talking about?" I try.

"My power is inside your blade," he says. "It is rightfully MINE."

I've never seen Ghazt so animalistic— monstrously menacing. Slobbery saliva splashes with each sharp-toothed snarl. His whiskers are rigid and as pointy as razors.

"I will have it back!" Ghazt roars.

I'm guessing that now is when the arm-chomping happens. Ghazt's mouth opens impossibly wide and he pounces! I've got no choice but to draw the Louisville Slicer. I'm whipping the blade out of its sheath, swinging it up, just as Ghazt is chomping down, and—

I feel pain, but it's not the sharpness of his fangs—it's an electric shock that reverberates through the blade, through the Cosmic Hand, through my entire body.

There is a sound like lightning splitting a great oak tree—and just as quickly as Ghazt's jaws came snapping down, they explode open again. Ghazt is blasted off his feet, flung fully backward—

Ghazt slams to the gangplank floor, stopping just short of my friends.

I gasp. *The Slicer. The Cosmic Hand. Together, they* rejected *him.*

Ghazt's head shakes sharply and he rises unsteadily. His eyes blink with confusion—then narrow as he looks first at the blade and then at the Cosmic Hand.

"That *thing* . . ." he growls. "It is more strange and more mysterious than I knew."

Yeah, I think. *I'm starting to realize that, too.*

"Y'know, this is maybe a discussion best had back indoors," I say, throwing a quick glance over the side. Ground rushes past, nearly fifty feet below. "Instead of out here, where— y'know . . . falling is a very distinct possibility."

Ghazt's face twists into a mask of resigned frustration as he eyes the blade and the Cosmic Hand. "I cannot retrieve it. The power you *stole* from me. I . . . I cannot take it back."

He steps forward—and the words that follow chill me to the bone.

"But I can still take your life . . ."

Just then, my friends jump in, leaping to my aid!

"Show some respect for your Grand Protector!" Evie shouts, leaping into the fray. She's on Dirk's back, clawing at him, trying to pull him off Ghazt.

"REAAARGH!"

Ghazt goes into pure special-attack mode—a Tasmanian-devil whirling dervish! Dirk, Quint, and June are flung from his body, hurled back up the gangplank.

And Evie is hurled into me.

The air explodes out of my lungs as she hits me square in the chest. Then we're both tumbling, out of control, end over end down the gangplank. One flip and my back slams into metal. Another and Evie's elbow jabs me hard in the side. One last flip and this time we hit nothing but empty air . . .

chapter sixteen

I'm covered head to toe in dirt and grime—and there's pain head to toe, too. I press my hand against the ground. Pebbles push into my bare palm as I sit up slowly, shaking out the cobwebs.

What just happened?

Oh right. Ghazt, gangplank, fighting, falling.

In the distance, the Mallusk is speeding away, leaving a destruction-filled crevice in its wake. All the dirt and dust makes me feel like I've fallen into some kind of old-timey Wild West town. Dirk would go nuts for it.

Except Dirk's not here. None of my friends are. My friends are back on board.

There's only one other person here . . .

If I have to be stranded out in the wasteland wilds, Evie is the *last* person I'd choose to be with. But, I suppose, the *last* person is better than *no* person.

I get to my feet, slowly at first—but then *very quickly* as Evie rises, swinging her weapon . . .

"Oh, c'mon!" I shout, drawing the Slicer as I jump back, deflecting the blow.

"You stole Ghazt's powers!" Evie barks. "You got us *both* stranded out here in the middle of nowhere! Everything was going fine on the Mallusk until you and your friends showed up!"

"Hey, for real," I say, "can we just dial it down a notch?"

Evie's breathing hard, ready to keep going. I lower the Slicer—only slightly.

"I walked right into that one," I say with a frustrated sigh. "No. I mean get back to the Mallusk. My friends are on board."

Evie's nose wrinkles at the word "friends," and I can tell I've hit a sore spot.

"Uh, yeah, duh, me too," she spits. "I have a Cosmic General to get back to? Also Smud, who's a close pal. And in case you've forgotten, I have an entire mall full of monsters to rule over. I mean . . . protect. Yeah, protect. Help protect. With Ghazt."

I roll my eyes. Even after surviving a near-fatal fall off a gigantic beast, all she can think about is ruling. Power.

And it's that thirst for power that got us into this mess.

I turn my back to Evie and start walking along the Mallusk's carved-out path. I don't need her. I've got my Slicer, the air in my lungs, and the blood in my veins. I'll be fine.

It takes an hour just to trek up and out of the crevice the Mallusk made. The sun is starting to set by the time I reach the narrow peak. It's like a jagged mountain ridgeline built from suburban rubble.

That's when I hear Evie's footsteps at my
back . . .

My ears guess she's a few paces behind.
Although—I actually have no idea how big a pace
is. Is it bigger than a click? Definitely smaller
than a league.

I don't want to look back—don't want to give
her the satisfaction.

But it's a treacherous, precarious walk.
And with the sound of every shaky step, every
strange footfall, I can't help but spin, expecting
to find Evie mid-attack. About to push me,
whack me, *something*.

And each time I spin, Evie stops, stiffens, and steadies herself for battle. It goes on like this for nearly an hour, until—

Enough! My nerves are fried to a crisp, OK? You can't keep acting like you're ready to strike at any moment.

Me?! What about you?!

"What *about* me?!" I shoot back.

"You keep spinning around like you're gonna knock me off the road!"

"'Cause you keep being about to strike!"

"'Cause you keep spinning!"

I sigh. "It's a chicken-or-the-egg thing."

"Who you calling chicken?"

"Uh-uh, nope," I say. "Don't try to Marty McFly me."

That gets her. After a long moment, a smile cracks her face.

"Look," I say with a tired sigh. "We'll never get back to the Mallusk like this. What about a temporary truce?" I say.

"How temporary you talking?" she asks.

"I dunno," I say with a shrug. "More than a moment, less than a lifetime."

"Combat?" Evie asks.

"On pause."

"Being enemies?"

"Still enemies," I say. "But a freeze on all being-enemies activities."

Evie scrunches up her nose, then taps her finger against her chin.

I groan. "I can't believe I have to be the adult when you are the *actual adult*."

"Fine," she says. "We'll be *civilized*, but you've got some explaining to do. It's time to lay *all* your cards on the table—even the jokers and those little instructional ones."

"Fine," I say.

She gets straight to the point. "The way you controlled those zombies with your silly charred baseball bat was way bigger—way *more*—than you did in the bowling alley . . ."

ZOMBIE GRAB!

"First of all—*Louisville Slicer*," I say. "It's called the Louisville Slicer."

"*The Louisville Slicer*," she mimics. "It now contains *all* of Ghazt's power. HOW?"

I wish Quint were here. Then we could do that BFF eye-beam thing again and he'd be all smart and help me know what to say. But maybe, perhaps, if I just think hard enough . . .

Imaginary BFF eye-beam thing*

*IMAGINARY QUINT'S EYE BEAM: Jack, you got this. Evie's already seen the power the Slicer wields. No need to hold back now.

*JACK'S EYE BEAM: Thanks, Imaginary Quint. I hope things are going OK on board the Mallusk and Ghazt hasn't eaten you.

"OK, Evie—I'll tell you," I say. "But you better give up your secrets in return."

Evie lets out a sarcastic huff, but nods her head: a yes.

So I tell her what went down, back when
Thrull chased me on the Tendrill . . .

Thrull gripped me with his Ghazt-tail-fused arm.

The tail merged with the Scrapken tentacle on my hand,
resulting in a burst of energy. And it became the Cosmic
Hand . . .

The power left the Cosmic Hand and entered the Louisville
Slicer.

But it didn't sap Thrull of all power—I control the undead, but he controls something else . . .

"And now," I say, holding up the Cosmic Hand, "this thing is a permanent glove. It's the only way I can wield the Slicer. Without it, I can't control the zombies. And also—"

I pause. I decide not to mention how it sort of *jacked in* to Thrull, and how I had a vision of him and saw him in the Tower. I don't mention what I felt when I grabbed hold of the Howler—how the Cosmic Hand allowed me to peek behind the curtain, see and feel and sense the *evil*.

" . . . And also, that's it," I finally say. "Yep. And also, that's it."

Evie leans forward. I'm not certain if she's intrigued, excited, or ticked off. "What do you mean, 'he controls something else'?"

We learned he can now control the ACTUAL dead. Skeletons.

Evie leans closer. "So you're saying you now control the zombies, and Thrull is a legit *necromancer* who leads a skeleton army?"

"That's pretty much the gist of it," I say with a shrug. "Now go," I say. "Your turn to spill. What are you and Ghazt actually *after*?"

Evie tilts her head, looking unsure. Finally, she begins. "Months ago, Ghazt and I set out in search of Thrull and the Tower. We boarded the Mallusk, hoping it would get us closer to the Tower. But it hasn't. And that has Ghazt . . . scared."

"Huh?" I ask. *"Scared?"*

"Scared that Thrull will actually finish the Tower," Evie continues. "Because if Ṛeżżőcħ *does* come, he'll kill Ghazt for not constructing and completing the Tower *himself.*"

"So . . . what? Ghazt's hiding out on the Mallusk, bossing around a bunch of weaker monsters?" I ask. "Because he's too terrified to do anything?"

Evie shakes her head and grins cruelly. "Oh, no. See, that was all *before*. Before what just happened. Before Ghazt learned that *you* had his power—and that he would never be able to get it back. So now, Jack . . ."

chapter
seventeen

We follow the Mallusk's path of destruction in silence.

But it's not silent *enough*. Because every few seconds I hear beeping. And it's coming from Evie. Or, more specifically, from Evie's Game Boy.

We trudge along the ridgeline, high above the massive canyon left in the Mallusk's wake, and I try to ignore the sounds. But I can't. She's playing *Dark Arts Tower Defense* and the music is *the most annoying*.

I try to drown out the beeps with noise of my own. I start whistling. And I'm not even good at whistling.

And if there was any chance that Evie was just accidentally annoying me, it becomes clear that she is definitely on-purpose annoying me because the louder I kinda-whistle, the louder she turns up the volume on her Game Boy.

I think I'm losing my mind.

"WILL YOU TURN THAT OFF!" I finally scream.

"No," she says flatly, still mashing the buttons. "Walking is the worst, and I need something to distract me."

"Then at least play it with the sound down!"

I can't believe it. I sound like a dad on a long car ride. *That* is what Evie has done to me.

"The sound helps me," she says.

I let out a grunt. "Helps you? You need *help* beating *Dark Arts Tower Defense*?"

In response, she just smacks the console against her hand. "This stupid boss! He's *impossible*."

"Give it to me." I stop walking and hold out my hand. "I've beaten that final boss more times than I can count!"

"Hold on a sec," Evie says, looking up from the game.

"For real," I say. "Just give it to me, and I'll take care of it."

"Seriously," she says. "There's something up ahead . . ."

Evie nods. "The worst."

"Finally. Something we can agree on."

"Sometimes when Ghazt isn't looking, I spray Febreze," Evie says.

I laugh. We both do. Then it's weird and we shut right up.

The smell comes from within this train station or the scattered train car graveyard beyond. It was already a mass of wreckage—the path cut by the Mallusk just punctuated it.

"Widow's Crossing Train Yard," I say. "Doesn't sound foreboding at all. Probably just—"

Sccccritch. Sccccritch.

The scratching sound shuts me up. We sneak through the station, following the foul odor and strange noise. Coming around an overturned ticket machine, the smell of evil hits me so hard I gag.

Neither of us are prepared for the mangled, monstrous mess lying on the train tracks.

SCRITCH, SCRITCH . . .

"It's one of those Mortar Monster things," I whisper. "From the rest stop."

One wounded claw is scraping the ground,

making a nails-on-chalkboard noise. It seems to be on its last legs. Which means it must have been dying for a while, 'cause it has a lot of legs.

Up close, it's even clearer that the Mortar Monster and the Pilot-Thing are a single entity. Conjoined. What happens to one happens to the other. They feel the same pain. And they're both feeling it bad now . . .

"Must have been caught beneath the Mallusk during the escape," I say softly. "Dragged for miles before being spit out here."

"Mallusk roadkill," Evie says with a shrug.

Sccc-Scccc-Sccriiiiitch.

I watch the Pilot-Thing's taloned hand claw at the ground. It's trying to say something, but its voice is all gurgled and wet.

"ME⋛CQ-€¥$ZZK . . ."

The Pilot-Thing wheezes and its head lifts. I follow its foggy, heavy-lidded eyes and realize it's checking out the Slicer.

"Sorry, buddy," I say, placing a protective hand around my Slicer. "This ain't for you."

The Pilot-Thing's cavernous mouth twists up into a strange, shifty smile. It speaks—and its voice is like something pulled from nightmares. It's the voice that beckons from beneath the bed after the lights go out.

The Pilot-Thing continues hissing. *"YESSSS. REACH THE MŒLÙSQÇÂL. I HOPE YOU DO. WE HOPE YOU DO."*

"What's this thing playing at?" Evie asks.

I'm not sure. But there is some part of me that must know; some part of me that won't leave without hearing what the creature has to say.

"YOU THINK YOU ARE SAFE ABOARD THAT CREATURE, YESSSS?" the Pilot-Thing rasps in pain. *"YOU ARE GRAVELY MISTAKEN. THE CREATURE HAS BEEN . . . COMPROMISED. YESSS. WONDERFULLY COMPROMISED. THERE IS A NEW RESIDENT IN CHARGE."*

The hairs on the back of my neck are prickling. My friends are on board. Mallusk City citizens are on board. If the Mallusk itself is compromised . . . My imagination jumps the tracks, going to dark, horrible places . . .

"What's that mean?" I ask. "TELL ME. NOW!"

The Pilot-Thing lets out a wet, scratchy, near-death cough. *"YOU WILL UNDERSTAND . . . WHEN IT REACHES ITS DESTINATION . . ."*

The Mallusk doesn't have a destination. It just goes.

HUMANS . . . ALWAYS SO SURE OF WHAT THEY KNOW . . . EVEN WHEN THEY KNOW NOTHING . . .

The Pilot-Thing coughs, hacking up a smattering of thick black goo. *"DO YOU RECALL ANY PERMANENT DAMAGE TO YOUR PRECIOUS MALLUSK? HM?"*

Evie's eyes catch mine. *Permanent damage?*

The Pilot-Thing beckons us. Evie doesn't move, but I reluctantly step closer—just barely. The Pilot-Thing's mouth opens slightly. It whispers something. I'm forced to take another step forward to hear.

"THRULL OWES YOU A GREAT DEBT," it says, speaking directly to me now. *"FOR YOUR INABILITY TO CONTROL YOUR NEWFOUND POWER."*

"How much debt we talkin'?" I ask. "Enough debt that he'll leave us alone and go away forever?"

The Pilot-Thing manages to choke out its next sentence. *"IT IS A DEBT HE WILL NEVER NEED REPAY."*

I have no idea what the Pilot-Thing is getting at. I'm turning the words over, when—

"AIEEE!"

I shriek, half in pain and half in surprise, as a sick grin crosses the pilot's dying face and one of the Mortar Monster's massive claws clamps down around my wrist.

Out of the corner of my eye, I see Evie sprinting away, turning a corner, gone.

I'd love to follow, but the claw tightens, and the Pilot-Thing pulls me close. *"WE TOLD YOU THE TRUTH. BUT IT WAS A TRADE. THE TRUTH, FOR YOUR LIFE. YESSS."*

I scrape and punch and push and kick, but the Mortar Monster's grip is impossibly rock-solid tight.

"WE WILL LET THE HOWLER HAVE THE PLEASURE OF DELIVERING YOUR FRIENDS, EVEN IF IT IS TOO FAR GONE TO ENJOY ITS REWARDS. BUT YOU, BOY, YOU ARE OURS."

Shock and confusion flood through me. "The Howler?" I choke out.

WOULD YOU THINK, FOR A MOMENT, THAT THOSE LOYAL TO THRULL ARE NOT IN COMMUNICATION?

THAT ONCE THE HOWLER TOOK CONTROL, NEARBY SERVANTS WOULD NOT FIND OUT?

WORD SPREADS—NOT QUICKLY ENOUGH FOR THRULL'S LIKING, BUT IT SPREADS.

Evie, the Howler is in control! It's the Howler that—

The monster's pincher squeezes my wrist, and the rushing pain silences me. **"YOU ARE ABANDONED BY YOUR HUMAN FRIEND."**

"She's not my friend," I manage to squeak out.

"WE WILL NOW DO WHAT SO MANY OF THRULL'S SOLDIERS FAILED TO DO. WHAT EVEN ȐEŻŻŐCH FAILED TO DO. AND WE WILL RECEIVE OUR REWARD IN THE DIMENSION BEYOND DIMENSIONS . . ."

I watch the Pilot-Thing, near-death, make its move. Long, talon-like fingers flash in the air! Curved nails stab into the Mortar Monster's meaty flesh, slicing it open. The Mortar Monster unleashes an earth-quaking cry as the Pilot-Thing jams its hand inside and *tugs*.

SNICK!
REEEARGH!

Nope, nope. Whatever you're doing, don't. Please!

Eww, that's gross.

The Mortar Monster's scream trails off as black and neon purple light begins to glow beneath its shell. There's a sizzling sound.

I've seen enough movies to know that this Mortar Monster has some sort of self-destruct inside it—and the Pilot-Thing just triggered it.

Ice-cold air floods out of the monster. Its body starts to crumple in on itself—like a can of soda being crunched and mashed. It's a sort of reverse explosion—the start of an inward detonation.

One huge, lobster-like claw grabs for me, finding the Cosmic Hand. Squeezing.

Furious pain explodes inside the Cosmic Hand, speeds through my body, shoots into my skull.

The monster crumples further as the self-destruct continues—snapping and popping. But its grip around the Cosmic Hand only grows tighter, and—

Something happens.

Suddenly, I'm in another world. A nothing place. Surrounded by nothing but darkness . . .

chapter eighteen

There's a strange weightlessness to my body.
I felt this same way, a year earlier, when the
King Wretch hijacked my brain—showing me
visions of possible futures, possible realities.

But this isn't a nightmare world.

This is a nothing world.

And in this nothing world, I have time to
think . . .

THRULL OWES
YOU A GREAT
DEBT. FOR YOUR
INABILITY TO
CONTROL YOUR
NEWFOUND
POWER.

Everything
was going fine
on the Mallusk
until you and
your friends
showed up!

My mind goes back. Before the Mallusk.
Before leaving Wakefield.

Back to the night Bardle died.

That's when I first connected to the dark
energy—the power to control and manipulate
the undead.

I pulled Ghazt's powers out of the tail and
that strange, cosmic energy filled the Scrapken
tentacle that covered my hand. It lived in that
hand, for a brief moment. And then that energy
and power was transferred into the Slicer. It
was drained from my hand and injected into
the Slicer, turning it the color of midnight: the
Midnight Blade.

After that, the Scrapken tentacle became a
permanent glove: the Cosmic Hand.

Ghazt's powers in the blade combined with the
Scrapken tentacle wrapped around my hand?
Those are two major forces uniting to form one
cosmic mega-weapon.

And that mega-weapon is the only way I'm able
to control the zombies . . .

Suddenly, a strange bolt of lightning—reverse
lightning, erupting through the ground—
appears in the distance of this nothing world
as the thought strikes my brain—
Alfred!

"Um, sorry," I say after a moment. "You scared me. Didn't know anyone else was, uh, here. Thought I had this astral plane all to myself. But . . . you *are* here, too? Right?"

Alfred glances around. "Apparently, I am, sir."

"You just appeared? And—wait!—you actually talk like a butler?! That's how you speak?"

"I speak exactly the way you imagine I speak," Alfred says. His voice is soft and flat and calm.

"Oh. OK. Um, can we chat? 'Cause I'm . . . I'm just really confused. Bardle and Warg taught me to control zombies. I speak, out loud, the things I want you guys to do, and then I swing the Slicer and you guys do those things. You follow the commands. Like, I dunno . . . 'ALFRED, BRING ME A CHAIR!'"

HEY!
Oh, thanks.

I look down at the chair, decide it's real enough to get comfy in, and lean back and continue. "But Alfred, back at the water park, I controlled you *without* the Slicer. That happened, right? I didn't make that up?"

Alfred is silent.

"See, I thought it was my brain reaching out—like the Force. That's what it felt like. But . . ."

"But . . . ?" Alfred asks.

"But it wasn't some sort of Jedi telepathy, was it?"

"Certainly not, sir," Alfred says. "You are *no Jedi*."

"OK, you don't have to sound so happy about it," I say. I look down at the Cosmic Hand. "So now I'm thinking . . . it was this. The Cosmic Hand. *It* delivered the commands—just like the Slicer delivers commands. I don't think there's any other-dimensional, zombie-controlling power *in me*. It's just . . . the Cosmic Hand and the Slicer, together—they, like, allow me to wield *that* power."

"Hmm," Alfred says.

"Without the Cosmic Hand, I could have sat up on Blargus's back all day long, trying to send thoughts and commands from my brain to yours—but nothing would have happened. Right?"

"Perhaps," Alfred says.

"So I used the Cosmic Hand and *only* the Cosmic Hand to control you . . . and after that, it began to change . . . The Cosmic Hand has been different. Felt different. Looks different! Makes *me* feel different. Do you think so?"

"I think whatever you think," Alfred tells me. "I am a figment of your imagination."

I shake my head. The Cosmic Hand is a bigger unknown than I ever realized: maybe the Biggest Unknown.

And I used that Biggest Unknown to grab the wounded Howler as it rocketed toward Quint. And the Howler felt its power. It knew, then, that it had found Jack Sullivan, the kid with the blade who stopped Thrull once before, half stopped him a second time, and generally just really gets on Thrull's nerves. The kid Thrull's forces were searching for . . .

But the Howler was injured. Too injured to fly off to the Tower and be all like, *"HEY, BOSS, FOUND THE LITTLE GUY! HE'S IN A BIG TRAVELING MALL. YOU SHOULD GO GET HIM!"*

And then . . . the Howler crashed into the Mallusk and died. End of story.

Right?

'Cause once it was dead, the fact that it had seen me, knew who I was—that was useless . . .

Right?

"Alfred . . ." I say. "The Pilot-Thing—it said the Howler is in control. But if that's true, then . . . the Howler can't be dead."

"I find no fault in that logic," Alfred says with a slight nod.

Suddenly, the Cosmic Hand pulsates
and vibrates! I'm understanding—and that
understanding is triggering something. Pain
shoots through the hand—and from that pain,
from that hand, comes clarity. I see—*I'm
shown*—what happened . . .

I rock slightly in the chair as a wave of dread
washes over me. "The Howler smashed into the
Mallusk, vines stretching, taking control. And
now it's taking the Mallusk to Thrull. Taking
all of us to Thrull . . ."

"*Us?*" Alfred asks.

"Oh," I say. "Right. I'm not on board. Not anymore."

"But I am. Thanks a lot for that one, *sir.*"

Great. Even my imaginary butler's got an attitude.

"I told Evie that Thrull's forces would have come for the Mallusk no matter what . . . but that's not true, is it? They came because they were searching for us, for *me*, after I killed Blargus, and after we escaped with Drooler."

Alfred's head lowers. "And everything you did after that, sir . . ."

I swallow. "All of it has helped Thrull . . ."

I have doomed everyone on board the Mallusk . . . I have doomed everything . . .

A gust of frigid air blows across this Nothing Land.

"Gotta go!" Alfred says, and he disappears in a puff of neon smoke. The colors fade, revealing . . .

Thrull.

Everywhere.

His monstrous face, vast and endless, covers the entirety of the astral plane's infinite sky. And he's laughing . . .

HA! HA! HA! HA! HA! HA! HA! H

Thrull's horrible, mocking laughter grows louder and louder, until—

SKREEE!!!

The Mortar Monster! It's crying out! Its pained shriek explodes from everywhere, all around me, like the world itself is screaming . . .

And Thrull's face *shatters*!

It explodes in a million jagged pieces as dazzling beams of light erupt from the darkness beyond, everything blazing, so bright I'm blinded, and then I see nothing at all . . .

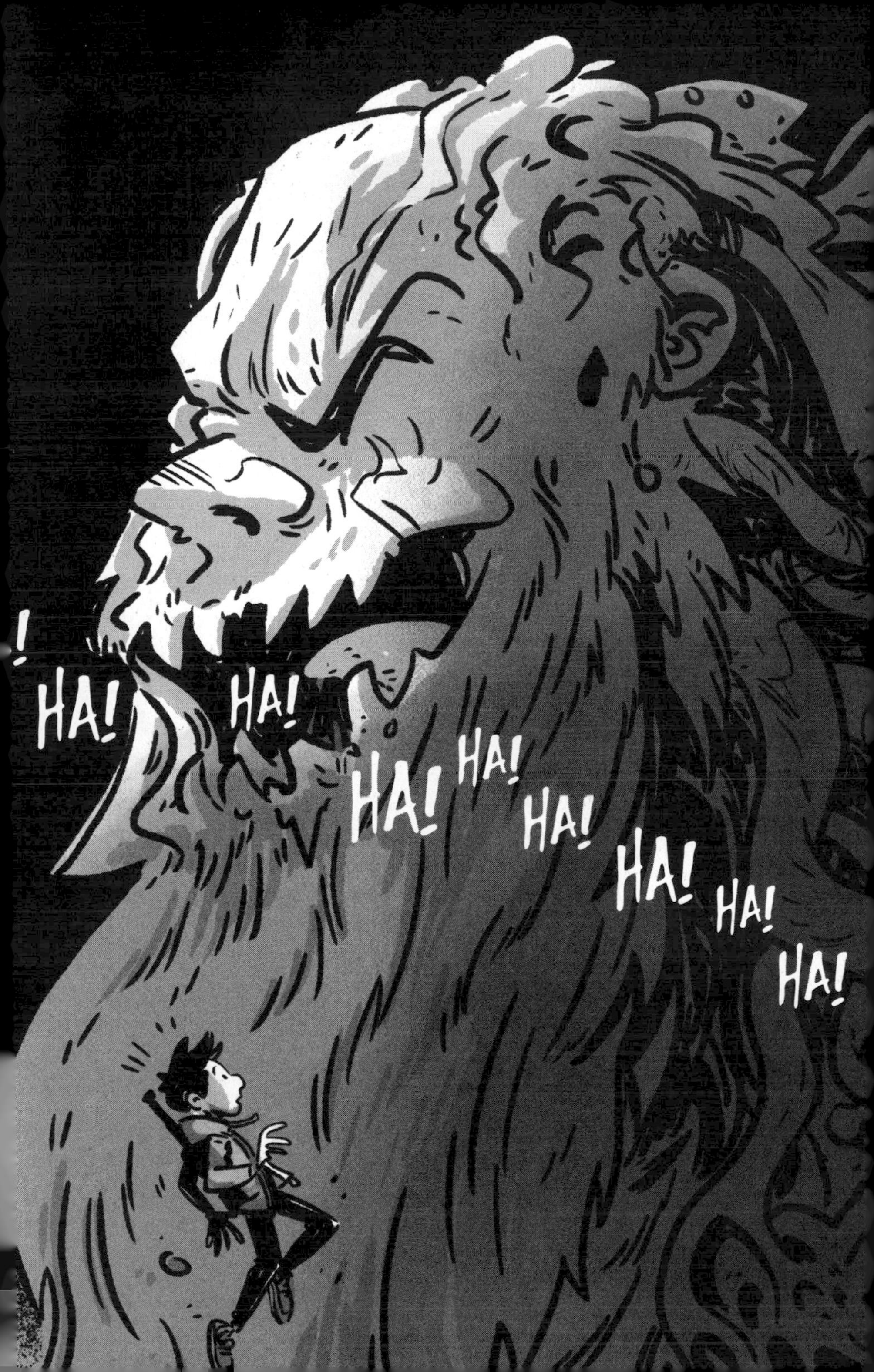
HA!
HA!
HA!
HA!
HA!
HA!
HA!
HA!

chapter nineteen

GET UP!

"OK! I'M AWAKE!" I shout.

"Just trying to help," Evie says with a shrug.

I squint up at her. "Wha . . . ? Was I . . . Am I alive?"

"Nope. You're totally dead right now."

"You're the worst," I say, slowly sitting up.

Evie chuckles. "I don't know *what* you were doing. You were mumbling a lot. And then you weren't doing anything at all—just breathing and drooling—for, oh, six hours. I played *a lot* of Game Boy."

"SIX HOURS?" I exclaim. "But . . . No, that can't be . . . It was just a few minutes. Then the Mortar Monster screamed, because its self-destruct thing had finished—"

"No. *I* finished it."

"But . . . you ran away . . ."

I look over at the Mortar Monster. It's dead—frozen, halfway through its folding-in-on-itself self-destruction. Evie's weapon juts out of it like a toothpick in a club sandwich.

"I don't like you, Jack. But I didn't do anything when Bardle died. So I did something this time."

I blink. "I don't like you, either, Evie."

Then suddenly everything I realized in the Nothing World comes flooding back to me. "Evie! The Howler is still alive! It's going to the Tower. I mean, it's controlling and taking the—"

"Mallusk?" Evie asks, sounding surprised.

"Yes! How'd you know I was gonna say that?"

"Mallusk?!" Evie exclaims.

"YES! But how'd you—"

"No!" Evie exclaims, yanking me to my feet and turning me.

MALLUSK!!

The Mallusk is sliding and roaring, no longer a steady, all-powerful bulldozer of a beast. It jerks left, then right—thrashing in pain.

And at the very front and center of the Mallusk—tiny, so tiny—something is happening. A burst of light. And then another.

The Mallusk jerks again now, careening in our direction. And I see that it's Yursl up there, near the Mallusk's horns.

VA-SHOOM!

Swirling energy—pinks and blues—erupt from the spot where Yursl is standing. "The Howler!" I gasp—but then there is another energy flare, erupting outward, and I reel back as the Howler is exploded through the air—

KAA-ZOOOSH!

The Howler crashes to the ground, landing in a pile of gnarled, rusty train track.

Yursl removed it from of the Mallusk's brain. Somehow. And destroyed it.

Sure is nice to have a conjurer around.

A thick storm of dirt fills the air as the Mallusk slides to a violent halt, like an airplane touching down with no landing gear. The Mallusk's front end is almost fully buried in the ground.

And then my friends are rappelling down the mountain-sized monster. And they're racing toward me, across the tangle of corroded train tracks. Johnny Steve hurries after them, trying not to trip on his little spy trench coat.

My head is spinning. I look to Evie—and she's just as confused as I am.

"Hey, friend!" Quint cries.

"What are you . . . ? How are you . . . ?" I start, but that's all I get out before June slams into me, lifting me off my feet, and Dirk and Quint are joining in.

"The Mallusk? You guys?" I manage to squeak out through Dirk's bear hug. "How . . . any of it? ALL OF IT?!"

"I believe I can best answer that," Johnny Steve says, sounding like Sherlock Holmes.

He gives Evie a quick nod, then adjusts her coat. He pats its side, beating out some of the dust that has gathered. Evie flicks his hand away.

"Now!" Johnny Steve begins. "Allow me to regale you with a story. I will do my best to recall the details exactly as I remember them."

"Buddy," June says. "There's not time for—"
But Johnny Steve just cocks an eyebrow, grins,
and begins narrating the tale of . . .

Smud, please remove this creature from my sight.

During one of Ghazt's "meet-and-greet-and-flatter" events, I planted the bug! However, the intelligence gathered was less than helpful...

AMERICAN CHEESE ISN'T *ACTUALLY* CHEESE, RIGHT?

But if it's not cheese, then what *is* it?

I feared I would obtain no valuable intel at all. But then...

235

239

240

NOW, I WILL HYPNOTIZE THE HOWLER TO MAKE IT STEER THE MALLUSK IN THE DIRECTION WE WANT IT TO GO . . .

YOU'RE GETTING VERRRRRY SLEEPY.

Next stop: Widow's Crossing Train Yard.

But as the Mallusk neared Jack, the Howler began to resist. Yursl could no longer keep the Howler subdued, so she summoned all of her conjurer energy and . . .

THUS CONCLUDES THIS EPISODE OF ...
JOHNNY STEVE:
SPY GUY!

I'm floored. For a few reasons. "Thank you,
Johnny Steve—" I begin, but not everyone is
feeling so grateful.

"OK, first," Evie says, "your campaign was *way more* cheaty and dishonest than ours. By, like, a lot. Yours had wiretapping!"

June sighs and nods. "Yup, yup. Still getting my head around that, too."

"And second," Evie says, looking thoroughly displeased, "there's one thing you failed to explain: Where did you plant the bug on me?"

REVEAL!

"And so, in conclusion . . ." Johnny Steve says. "Evil stopped! Though we still don't know what caused the Howler to target the Mallusk in the first place, after so many months without even a whiff of an attack."

I look down at the Cosmic Hand. I'm about to tell my friends that *I* triggered everything, when—

"Evil *not* stopped," June says. "Jack, after knocking you off the Mallusk, Ghazt went to work: he told all the monsters that you were dead, but in the interest of democracy, the election would still be held. And—thanks to Grand Protector Law #789—no voting for dead humans. Which means . . ."

"Ghazt's gonna make the monsters vote," I say. "For him."

"Bingo," June says.

"And if he wins . . ." Quint starts.

"Drooler is lost," Dirk says softly.

"Evil not stopped for another reason," I say, recalling my vision in that Nothing World and now knowing exactly what it means. "Thrull knows where we are. And if the Howler is no longer bringing us to him—then *he's* coming to *us* . . ."

chapter twenty

We march back to the wounded Mallusk, passing the Howler's broken body on the way. Yursl sags against the Mallusk's hide, looking like she just ran thirty-eight half-marathons. Or nineteen full ones, even.

Her skin is nearly see-through as she raises her head to look at Quint. "The Howler is dead. The Mallusk is free. But, it will be a long time before I can summon power like that again. I've passed you the ball . . . You must sink the shot."

"Thank you, Yursl," Quint says.

Yursl summons just enough strength to throw an arm around Quint. "You now have all you need to do what must be done," she says.

"And we will get it done," I say, sounding way more confident than I feel.

We leave Yursl to rest and enter the mall— a mall that feels very different than the one I tumbled off nine hours earlier.

What I see is a world under Ghazt's rule. And it's mean and scary. It reminds me of the Pride Lands at the end of *The Lion King*, when Simba returns and Scar has been an unstoppable overlord for years.

Also, it's just *annoying*. All our rad campaign signs have been torn down or covered up. In the hours since I was gone, Ghazt must have gone wild at Sir Prints-A-Lot, because the mall is plastered with really tacky photos of the big guy baring his teeth in what I guess is *supposed* to be a smile but actually looks like the "before" photo for some supercharged cavity-cleaning service.

June shakes her head. "What a cheeseball . . ."

I shoot a glance at Evie, who shrugs. "Wasn't part of my campaign strategy. Still—they're cool photos."

The first floor is empty of monsters—except for Smud. He's at the Victory Geyser, which looms ahead, with one hand on the lever.

"Things are going to start happening fast now," Quint says. He grips his conjurer's cane tight.

Smud pulls the lever and the floor rumbles as the geyser powers up. I walk quicker, taking the escalator stairs three at a time.

Ghazt stalks back and forth at the edge of his Food Court headquarters. "No orderly lines!" he barks. "No one cares about orderly lines! Just vote!"

Thousands of monsters are pushed up against the clear plastic railings that overlook the main rotunda and the stage. They are just moments away from throwing their ballot balls into the Victory Geyser. Each monster grips two ballot balls. On one, a hand-drawn rat. On the other, a hand-drawn me.

"Throw your ballots in now!" Ghazt orders. "Anyone who delays will be thrown in next."

Smud calls up, "But sir, the Victory Geyser is not quite—"

The monsters freeze.

I push my way to the third level railing,
directly across from Ghazt. Nearby monsters
step back, giving me and my friends space. From
above and below, monsters peer over the railing,
trying to see what's happening.

Down on the ground level, Smud shrieks. His
skates go out from under him and he flops on his
butt. "Ahh! That kid is back from the dead! He's
a zombie! Quick, Ghazt—control him with your
controlling powers!"

June groans. "He can't do that anymore, remember? Pay attention, Smud."

"No, YOU pay attention!" Smud shouts.

"I am."

"Well, good," Smud says. "Carry on, then."

"I'm trying," June sighs.

"ENOUGH!" Ghazt slaps the railing and glares at me. "I thought I was done with you, Jack . . ."

I feel the monsters watching me. They look overwhelmed. Understandable: in the past few hours, a lot has happened—culminating in their home doing a faceplant into the ground and a human kid with a baseball-bat sword marching in like some wannabe-king returning from the dead to claim his rightful throne.

Man, I am *so* Simba right now.

"Before you vote," I say, "you're getting a closing statement. From me, Jack Sullivan, candidate for mayor and totally *not-dead* kid."

I grip the railing and take a deep breath. "You need to know who and what you're voting for, *exactly*. Ghazt told you it was safety. But there is no safety. The Howler was delivering the Mallusk to the Tower . . . to Thrull. The Howler is dead now, but Thrull knows everything. And he's coming."

The monsters gasp. Then erupt—

June steps to the railing beside me. "We've told you the truth all along!"

I gulp. I don't want to do this. Not one bit. But these monsters deserve honesty. The lies have to end.

"No . . ." I say, trying to keep my voice steady. "We haven't told you the truth. Not all of it."

"Huh," Evie mutters. "Didn't see that coming."

"Jack," June starts. "What are you—"

"I didn't know it . . ." I continue. "But I left out something big: *I'm* the reason you're all in danger. It's my fault."

I can feel the tension in the monsters around me. I grip the railing tighter. "I've been telling you a fight is coming—a fight you can't hide from . . ."

I look down at the Cosmic Hand. *What powers does it hold that I don't understand? What path was I placed on when the Scrapken wrapped itself around me? What did I unknowingly agree to when I took Ghazt's power from Thrull's arm?*

I didn't even think to ask these questions before. I just acted. And now . . . here we are. In a bad, bad spot.

I try to continue, but my voice is hoarse. It doesn't have that authoritative cosmic warlord boom that Ghazt's does.

I glance at June. Her face is a jumble of confusion and fear—but there's also trust there. She hands me one of the PA microphones, and I give her a quick nod of thanks.

Suddenly, all the monsters are talking at once. Even with the aid of the PA microphone, I have to shout to be heard. "I could have kept that information from you. And you would have never known. *But you deserve the truth! You deserve a leader who will tell you the truth!*"

Farther down the railing, a hulking orange monster shouts, "You, human, are no leader!" Her eyes catch mine—and I look down.

I deserved that. I'm not a leader. At least not now, not yet—and maybe never . . .

"I know," I say. "I'm not that person. Which is why . . ."

"No, June," I say. "No huddle-up. I meant it."

Confusion shoots through Mallusk City's citizens like a bolt of electricity.

Ghazt's booming voice erupts over the babble. "That's that!" he shouts. "Jack's out, I win. And if the boy is right and Thrull now approaches, then you all know what must be done!"

The monsters look even more confused. "We do?" one asks.

"You must submit!" Ghazt punches a fist
into his grubby paw like what he's saying is
courageous and strong, when it's actually the
total opposite.

"But you're supposed to protect us!" a monster
shouts.

AND I AM! BY
ORDERING YOU TO SUBMIT
TO THRULL TODAY AND
BECOME HIS SERVANTS, I
AM KEEPING YOU SAFE. AND
IF YOU'RE NOT HAVING FUN,
I WILL COME GET YOU,
PROMISE.

JUST GIVE IT
A FEW WEEKS AND
YOU'LL PROBABLY
LIKE IT.

Ghazt sounds he's trying to convince a nervous
kid that they're *really* gonna enjoy sleepaway
camp, they just have to give it a fair chance.

"You're not coming with us?" another monster
asks.

"Me? No, no. I will bravely journey out the back
door. So that I am in a better position to come get

you later, if you don't like it at Thrull's. Which you totally will."

"HOLD ON!" I bark. "Ghazt, you're not mayor just yet."

"I'm the only candidate," Ghazt reminds me.

"Not so fast," I say. "I suspend my campaign. And nominate Johnny Steve in my place."

The monsters all look at Johnny Steve. A collective "Um . . ." comes from the crowd—Johnny Steve included.

"The secret spy?" one monster asks.

"Johnny Steve proved his bravery! He proved he's on the side of right by getting you to safety when the Mortar Monster attacked, monitoring Evie, and tracking us down," I say. "Plus, he's got this rad trench coat and fedora."

Johnny Steve edges forward. "Ahem. Well, I, um, I humbly accept this honor. Unfortunately, I'm a little caught off guard and—hoo—quite nervous, so if you could just bear with me for an hour or two while I gather my thoughts . . ."

June hurries forward, snatching the PA mic from my hand. "Heya, June Del Toro here, newly appointed campaign manager for nominee Johnny Steve, the private eye with an eye on the future! You must make a choice. NOW."

"VOTE FOR ME AND STAY ALIVE!" Ghazt booms. "AND LIVE COMFORTABLY AS SERVANTS!"

I scan the crowd. I can see it on the monsters' faces—I can even see it on the monsters who don't really *have* faces: they don't know who to trust, what to believe, or what to do.

"The choice is yours," I start to say, when suddenly—

BOOM!

Old Navy erupts! Aéropostale explodes! One massive blast blows a wide hole in the lower level's wall, raining down chunks of concrete, steel, and plastic. The shock wave tears through the mall.

What was once the home of board shorts galore is now just a jagged, gaping hole. And through that hole, we see an army. Thrull's army.

They are crossing the tangled graveyard of trains and track, marching for the mall.

And we're out of time.

chapter twenty-one

The thin smoke that follows the explosion drifts through the mall. It's like a fog that hangs over the Mallusk, amplifying the eerie silence that follows.

As that fog clears, the advancing enemy comes into full view.

And it is *not* a nice view.

This isn't just one division or one single squad of Thrull's army, like the swarming Howlers or the raging Mortar Monsters. This is more. *Much more.* And Thrull himself is leading this assault . . .

We can't see him yet, but we can hear him. His every word is a thunderous boom that echoes across the steel train graveyard beyond . . .

Hearing Thrull's voice again—not via some awful vision or a cryptic note wrapped in a nightmare but here, in the flesh—gets my adrenaline stampeding.

Thrull's voice booms. *"This day, the boy Jack Sullivan will die! This day, the creature called Drooler will die! But I will allow the rest of you to live! You will have the honor of aiding in the Tower's construction."*

The citizens of Mallusk City are frozen.

At first, I think it's fear that keeps them from fleeing. But it's worse than that: they're *listening. Considering.* Processing Thrull's vile proclamations and promises. I gulp. If he offers free pizza, we're done for.

"Now come!" he urges. *"Join me in ushering in the new age of Ṛeżżőcħ!"*

Above us, below us, the monsters look from Ghazt to Johnny Steve and then back to Ghazt.

And then, all at once, they cast their votes . . .

The monsters throw their ballot balls over the sides! The balls tumble into the Victory Geyser's huge, funnel-shaped tub, pinging, ponging, then finally swirling down into the hole at its base.

My friends step beside me.

The Victory Geyser lights up. A rainbow of pulsing colors as the ballots are counted.

BOOM! Another monstrous artillery blast rocks the mall. And another . . .

But despite the explosive assault, no one takes their eyes off the geyser. It counts and counts, and then—

DING! A sound like a giant toaster popping.

Suddenly, blue light flickers. A sort of hologram appears, projected onto the side of the geyser. It's that TV host, Harvey Cool Hair.

"Ohmygosh!" June squeaks. "It's him!"

"He's not real!" I say.

"But still!"

Announcing the winner of this year's *Late Teen Star* . . . He's hot, he's cool, he is . . . JOHNNY STEVE!

"No!" Evie cries.

The change happens instantly—the fastest transfer of power in election history.

The electrified defenses surrounding Evie and Ghazt's Food Court fortress spark once, then power down. The gates open with a heavy clang.

Evie and Ghazt are in control no longer. The loot—and Drooler—now belongs to Johnny Steve.

"We did it!" June shouts.

But any triumphant feelings are cut short as Ghazt leaps off the Food Court, over the Victory Geyser, and lands nearly on top of me.

His hide is heaving and his eyes are alight with fury as he stalks toward me. "I should have killed you for real," he snarls. "I still can . . ."

"And that power *can* still be yours," Evie says softly—almost timidly. "You just need to take it . . . Take it from Thrull."

Ghazt looks around: at the hundreds of monsters who did *not* vote for him, at the Slicer in my Cosmic Hand, and at the three zombies I control.

Then he hits me.

But it's only his shoulder, slamming into mine as he smashes past me, pushing through the sea of monsters. He lashes out with his rat paw, slicing a huge "Vote for Ghazt" banner in two. The torn pieces drift to the floor.

Evie and I hold a long look, then she follows him.

"OK," Johnny Steve says. "Now, as your mayor—"

Thrull's voice booms from beyond the walls of the mall. *"Do we agree on terms? Will you serve me, and live to see Ṛeżżőch come to this land?"*

Johnny Steve quickly wades through the monsters—his electorate, his voters, the community he is now responsible for. We follow him to a large outdoor terrace, overlooking the train graveyard behind. He peeks his head out and shouts, "NO DEAL, THRULL!"

The monsters cheer.

"*I'm sorry! I don't think I heard you!*" Thrull's voice booms.

"He didn't expect that, did he?" Johnny Steve says, raising his arms in a V for victory.

"*NO, I AM SERIOUS! I CANNOT HEAR YOU AT THIS DISTANCE!*" Thrull says.

Oh.

"Try this," June says, tossing Johnny Steve a Rockin' Ruby's karaoke boom box. He flips the on switch, then once more—

NO DEAL!

"Do you think he heard us that time?" Quint asks after a moment.

I shrug.

"Ahem. Um. Thrull, did you hear us that time?" June says into the Rockin' Ruby's mic.

"Indeed, I did. And my response: you shall all be destroyed this day."

"Sounds about right," I say.

"Hey, guys . . ." Dirk says, looking thoroughly done with this awkward back-and-forth. "Can we get Drooler now? Please?"

Quint answers for all of us. "Yes, Dirk. It's about time."

Moments later, we're marching toward the Food Court. Johnny Steve's voice booms from the Rockin' Ruby speakers the whole time, and there is a frenzy of action and movement around. "Everyone! To the parking garage! We will ride the carapaces to safety!"

Evie and Ghazt's fortress is littered with food scraps and hunks of crusted cheese. The stench of Ghazt is thick, but I barely notice. I'm too busy watching Mayor Johnny Steve open Drooler's strange, otherworldly cage.

No one says a word as Johnny Steve removes Drooler from the cage and gently hands him to Dirk.

REUNITED AND
IT FEELS SO GOOD!

For a brief moment, I forget about the enemy at the gates. I forget about the fight that's only moments away. It seems like we all do. We just watch Dirk hug his little buddy, watch the joy on his face as the moment washes over him . . .

During our road trip, we learned Dirk's pre-apocalypse life was, in some ways, filled with broken promises. But Dirk's promise to Drooler . . . it never broke.

"Get comfy, bucko," Dirk says to Drooler. He slings his sword and sheath over his back, then sets the little guy on the sword's hilt—his rightful home. "But not too comfy. We're about to need you, big time."

"We'll hold off Thrull as long as we can," Quint says to Johnny Steve.

"Now get outta here, duder," June says. "No big good-byes, 'cause I'll be seeing you again."

Johnny Steve nods—and then he's gone.

An empty slushie tank lies in a pool of sticky orange syrup on the floor. Dirk flicks a gigantic rat hair off the tank, then picks it up and throws it over his shoulder. With the help of his belt and some shoelaces, he turns the tank into a makeshift backpack. Drooler, perched above it, drips Ultra-Slime into the tank.

Dirk says, "I'll meet you guys downstairs . . ."

Drooler and I are gonna get Ultra-Slime flowing through this whole mall—just in case . . .

chapter twenty-two

"Very funny," June says, squinting to see the approaching enemy.

PFHOOM!

A bone bomb lands a hundred feet from us. Skeletons rise, taking on mangled new forms.

"Hey, guys, I didn't miss any of the good stuff, did I?" Dirk asks, suddenly appearing at our side, crouching down. Drooler is fast asleep on the sword's hilt—they must have been busy.

Dirk peers through the exploded wall. "Oh man, there is no good stuff, huh. Is that a Dozer out there? Be great if we could finish the 'good guys escape' thing before that gets any closer."

I pull my camera from my bag and peer through a new high-powered lens—thanks, mall Best Buy! I get a quick glimpse of the skeleton soldiers now marching forward. I pull the lens, zooming in further, twisting until it focuses—

And I zero in on Thrull's face.

He sits atop a throne of bone and vine, carried by skeletal soldiers.

He's looking more arrogant than ever. Like he's already won. He must think a wounded, half-dead Mallusk stranded in a rusted railway graveyard is easy pickings.

On any other day, that smugness would

grind my gears. But today, it gives me hope.

Because the longer he thinks he's got this in the bag, the longer Johnny Steve has to lead everyone to safety.

"Thrull's in the back," I say, returning to cover behind the wall. "But I doubt he stays there."

"I especially like Dirk's part of the plan," I say. "That's extra important."

Dirk gives Drooler a gentle shake. "Rise and shine, little buddy," he says as he sets Drooler on the edge of the slushie-slime backpack. Drooler's eyes blink open. He is, once again, a faucet of Ultra-Slime.

"It is time," Quint says, "to apply the slime." He dunks both tips of the grabber atop his conjurer's cane, careful to avoid any of its gizmos or tech. June goes next, swirling arrows, dunking sparklers, and dipping who-knows-what-else-is-in-her-fanny-pack in the slime.

I summon Alfred, Glurm, and Lefty. "Take a dunk, dudes," I say, and with a swing of the Slicer, their weapons go in.

June's walkie-talkie hisses. "Mayor Johnny Steve here! We are on the move!"

"Well," I say. "Guess we better get on with it."

Dirk slaps me on the back. He's grinning. With Drooler returned, it's like he's fully himself again. *More than himself.*

"Race ya!" Dirk shouts, and with that, we burst outside, onto a battlefield littered with train car husks and rusted steel, crashing headlong into Thrull's army of the dead . . .

Our two forces collide with a deafening crack. Drooler's Ultra-Slime does everything it's supposed to—and more.

"Missed you, buddy!" Dirk says. Drooler just chirps as Dirk's blade flashes, chopping through the surrounding horde. Drooler's Ultra-Slime splashes the enemies, burning away the vile vines that animate them and allow them to fight.

"Stay back!" Quint barks, skewering a particularly quick-moving skeleton soldier. Each

jab of his cane's Ultra-Slime-slathered tips
disables an enemy.

"June! Behind you!" I shout as I jam the Slicer
through a leaping skeleton.

June wheels. With a flick of her wrist, a deck
of Uno cards pops out from Blasty's underside;
another flick and the cards are rifled outward,
each one trailing Ultra-Slime.

A Dozer is barreling toward us. Its savage hands smack Thrull's skeleton soldiers aside, scattering them by the dozens.

"Alfred, Lefty, Glurm!" I shout, ripping the Slicer out of a falling skeleton soldier and swinging it toward the Dozer. "Take it down!"

My Zombie Squad surges forward—leaping, climbing, attacking! But the Dozer is only a servant of Thrull's evil. It is not dead, so the Ultra-Slime does no damage.

SKLUTCH!

But together, the zombies batter the beast just enough that when June barks, "GET DOWN!" there is hope.

June's arm jerks and a dozen smoke globes rocket into the Dozer's gaping maw. Its throat bulges, its eyes pop, and then the beast falls. Red and yellow smoke pour from its mouth.

We spin, half-blinded, not sure what will

come next. Suddenly, three skeleton soldiers leap through the cloud, clawing at Drooler! Their hands sizzle, vines melting, but still they pull.

"Nah," Dirk says, jerking back, yanking Drooler from their grasp. "Just got my buddy back. Not losin' him to you bony bozos."

Dirk jams his sword into the slushie tank, swirls it like he's charging a special move, then unleashes ultimate Ultra-Slime destruction . . .

The tidal wave of Ultra-Slime decimates a dozen soldiers. The bones of the already-were-dead-and-would-have-stayed-that-way-if-it-weren't-for-Thrull-being-the-*worst* are piling up. It's starting to feel like we could really win this . . .

And Thrull, still on his throne, looks furious.

Over the sounds of combat, Quint shouts, "Is that it? Is that all you can conjure, Saruman?"

"Quint!" I yell. "Why did you have to say that?! Don't quote *The Two Towers*! That's what the old king dude says right before the big orc—"

"Uruk-hai," Quint corrects me.

"—right before that Uruk-hai guy blows open the wall and messes everything up!"

And that's exactly what Thrull does next: messes up everything.

One sound rises above everything else.

A pained, monstrous roar.

I turn, looking to where the Howler lies dead. Vines are exploding through the ground surrounding its corpse.

My eyes shoot from the Howler to Thrull.

His long bone-whip arm withdraws from the ground—then jams in again! Metal track and rocky ground erupt. The vines find the Howler once more, and it screeches louder.

The Howler's body practically melts; flesh and scales and organs fall away, leaving only the skeleton structure underneath. Rising like a tidal wave is—

-The Bone Howler!-

REEEE-
AARGGHHH!

With a tremendous snap, the Howler is ripped
toward Thrull. And at the same moment, Thrull
leaps from his seat, meeting the Howler in the
middle of the battlefield. Thrull lands atop the
beast.

"Whoa," Dirk says. "That was pretty cool."

June frowns. "Really, dude?"

Dirk shrugs. "It was."

"So . . . it appears Thrull has a steed now," Quint says.

I gulp. "I think I'll be in the bathroom for this next part."

"How about we all go inside?" June says. Then, sharply, "*Now.*"

No one argues. No one ever argues when a monster like Thrull is barreling toward you atop a vine-powered Bone Howler . . .

chapter
twenty-three

But things aren't *all* bad.

Inside, the mall is empty of Mallusk City citizens. Evacuating thousands of monsters is no small feat, but the new mayor seems to be managing it.

"Johnny Steve!" June barks into her walkie-talkie. "Are you out of the mall yet?"

"Progress is being made!" Johnny Steve chirps. "We are atop the carapaces now and winding our way through the parking garage."

"Hey, friends," Quint says. "By my estimation, we have roughly nineteen seconds until the big bad arrives . . . Let's make 'em count!"

Quint's estimation is good. I count twenty-two seconds—twenty-two seconds later that Thrull, atop the Bone Howler, charges into the mall.

I watch, hidden, as the Howler lands with two tons of terrifying force, hitting the ground like some sort of malevolent monster truck.

The mall quakes. Bits of ceiling fall. An escalator crumbles.

Thrull, atop the beast, scans the area. He oozes nothing but calm—but man, how I want to make him ooze something else. (His insides!)

"Cowards—" Thrull starts to say, before he hears the glass shattering above him—

The Loot Globe splits open, showering Thrull and his steed in Ultra-Slime. The Bone Howler recoils, shaking off burning vines. Thrull rips a smoldering vine clump from his shoulder.

"Alfred, Lefty, Glurm—now!" I shout, swinging my slicer. My Zombie Squad bursts out from behind Auntie Anne's!

Alfred jams his long umbrella into the Bone Howler, staggering the beast. Glurm and Lefty are about to plant their weapons in Thrull when his bone-whip snaps, and—

You'll pay for that, I think as Quint and I make it back down to the bottom level, meeting Dirk and June.

Just then, June's walkie-talkie hisses and Johnny Steve announces, "The first carapaces are now exiting the parking garage!"

Thrull glances at the walkie in June's hand.

"Uh-oh," I say.

"Yeah, probably not good that Thrull heard that," June agrees.

Thrull climbs down from the Bone Howler and says two words in the language of Ṛeżżŏcħ.

"ðĕşa Użqŭl·."

The Bone Howler barks in response to his master's command, then stomps outside and takes off at a gallop, headed for the rear of the mall.

"It's going for Johnny Steve," I say. "And the monsters.

I glance at my friends.

"We'll head off the Bone Howler," Dirk says.

Quint flicks a switch on his conjurer's cane. "We will keep them safe. *This* will keep them safe."

I shoot Quint a look. He shoots it back. Both of us . . .

*JACK'S EYE BEAM: Watch yourself, buddy!
*QUINT'S EYE BEAM: Be careful, friend!

And then Quint and Dirk are off, racing for the parking garage's exit.

June looks my way. "Hey, Jack, I'm sorry, but . . . I didn't hang around that weird kiosk as much as everyone else. So . . . is Quint a wizard now? Is that what's happened here?"

"No, no, don't be ridiculous," I say. "He's just an intern. Thoroughly unpaid."

June *hmm*s then nods. "All right, then."

WAKKT!

Thrull's bone-whip cracks, slicing through the floor of the mall. The Mallusk shudders.

So it's me and June—versus Thrull. And, in the distance, more of Thrull's soldiers approaching.

I raise the Slicer. June readies Blasty.

"We got this, right?" I ask.

"Totally," she says while shaking her head, 'no.'

But then, the monorail . . . I hear it before I see it. And when I do it see it, it's too late . . .

Thrull's bone-whip coils around me, yanking me off my feet! The sudden jerk of the monorail causes the Slicer to slip from my hand. Thrull's bone-whip jerks me upward and I slam, face-first, into the speeding monorail.

I manage to slap the Cosmic Hand onto the underside of the car so that I hang suspended, feet dangling. Glancing back, I watch the Slicer bounce across the floor and roll beneath the Foot Locker's half-lowered metal gate. *Crud.*

With a sudden whoosh, the monorail follows the curving track, whipping through the mall at *way too high* a speed. I get my other hand up onto the monorail floor.

Above me, the car shudders and seesaws as Ghazt and Thrull clash inside the tiny, too-confined space. It's like a cage match held inside a closet.

Ghazt roars, "I will take your power!" He hurls the full weight of his rat body onto Thrull. The car shakes and the track swings as they slam to the floor.

But Thrull only laughs. "Ghazt . . . This is a delightful surprise. I came here merely to destroy the boy and Drooler. But now I see there is something else of value on board . . ."

I spot the Victory Geyser—that means we're careening back toward the center of the mall. "Hey, uh, bad guys!" I call up. "This sounds like a Thrull and Ghazt problem, so if it's cool, I'm just gonna hop off and—"

"Not so fast!" Ghazt snarls, and his heavy paw slaps down onto my hand. "You won't be getting off yet!"

"How about we *all* exit this absurd conveyance?" Thrull says, then—

SNAP!

A huge crack suddenly appears in the monorail—and I realize Thrull's bone-whip has just slashed clean through the track. At once, it's collapsing—the track crumbling, the monorail tilting, everything plunging to the ground.

I leap off—aiming for anything soft. I get lucky—and land on a giant Build-A-Bear teddy. I roll into a sitting position just in time to see Ghazt hit the floor.

An instant later, the falling monorail lands. The entire weight of the car comes crashing down on Ghazt.

Thrull laughs.

Behind him, dozens of skeleton soldiers are stepping into the mall. *Talk about bad to worse.*

I spot Ghazt, curled beneath the crashed monorail. His body is twisted all wrong. Strange blood—part rat, part monster—begins to pool around him.

"COME HERE!" Thrull barks.

His bone-whip snaps out, seeking and finding Ghazt. It tightens. Thrull yanks Ghazt up into the air and then slams him back down so hard that the mall quakes.

Huh? I think. *What information is he talking about?*

Thrull kneels down, snarling. "I have big plans, Ghazt. To complete them, I need what is in your head. And I will get it . . ."

I don't understand any of that. But now's not the time to figure it out.

Out of the corner of my eye, I spot Evie. She's been watching from the top level. She must know Ghazt is done for. And she must know that means she's done for, too, because she turns and runs.

Ghazt continues to twitch on the ground beneath Thrull, who now turns his attention to me. "And Jack. Do not think I've forgotten about you. You, I have no use for. You, I will simply destroy."

I look around for help. But I don't see anyone.

Then, June's voice behind me says, "Jack, we won the election. And that means . . . it's party time."

"I'm sorry, what?" I manage.

"Party time. Y'know—*get down!*"

"I really don't know what—"

I realize what June means a split second after
I hear the boom.

I throw myself to the ground, hands over my
head, as—

It all seems to happen in slow motion, like I'm watching an instant replay.

I understand now what Dirk and Drooler were doing before we squared off against the skeleton army. Gallons upon gallons of Drooler's slime have been poured into the Victory Geyser, turning it into a massive Ultra-Slime cannon.

Wet confetti explodes outward. And then come the ballot balls. Thousands of them, each one now an Ultra-Slime-soaked projectile, screaming toward Thrull and his army.

I see Thrull's bone-whip tighten around Ghazt, ripping him upward, just as—

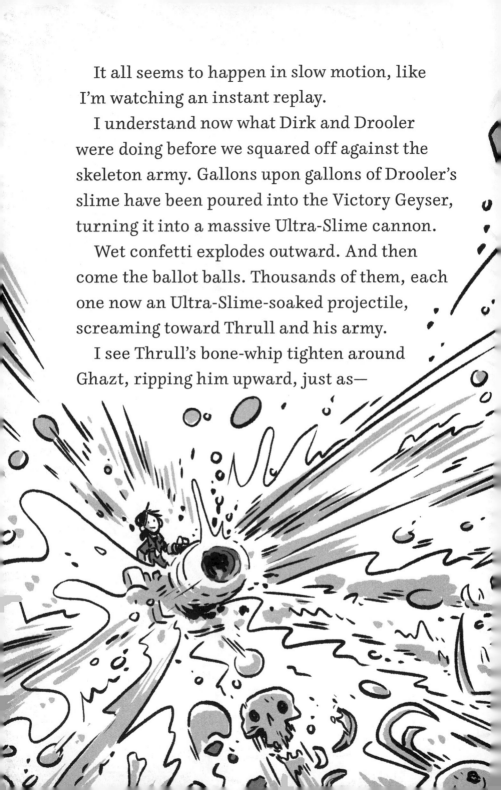

June just ended it. *All of it*. Game over.

Steam streams off the vines. The army falls, collapsing in a heap of smoking bone.

June just won *everything*. She—

"*No . . .*" The word escapes my lips. And I want so badly to not have said the word that I almost throw my hands over my mouth.

The steam clears and I see Ghazt—suspended midair. His tail smacks softly against the floor.

And Thrull, still standing, bone-whip tight around Ghazt. He used the whip to yank Ghazt up and hold him in place: a giant rat shield.

June's smile gives way to horrified shock. That was it: our big shot. And it has been shot. And the shot didn't land.

My eyes dart. The Slicer. I see it, so very far away, inside the Foot Locker.

Thrull sees it, too. "Nothing you can do without your little stick, is there?"

But there *is* something I can do. Alfred, Lefty, and Glurm are in the mall, somewhere. And . . .

I glance down at the Cosmic Hand. I could do what I did at Aqua City. I could control them with *only the Cosmic Hand*. I could, maybe, send them screaming toward Thrull with their Ultra-Slime-splattered weapons.

But rushing through my mind is a tidal wave of memories. Memories and mistakes. Everything that went wrong since I used the Cosmic Hand, alone, to command Alfred. So many things I did without thinking . . .

Grasping the vine that allowed me to see Thrull—and also allowed Thrull to see me.

Controlling Alfred—and revealing our location to Thrull's forces.

Grabbing the Howler—and setting the Mallusk on a pained journey toward our enemy . . .

All that I did has led us here. To this moment.

Maybe Dirk and Quint can defeat the Bone Howler. Maybe the monsters will escape on the carapaces. Maybe June can get out of this mall.

But me?

As Thrull steps toward me, icy cold radiating off his bone-whip and rushing over me like impending death, I'm not certain that I'll make it out.

No. I'm closer to certain that I *won't*.

The Cosmic Hand pulses once, and I know what I have to do . . .

chapter twenty-four

I throw myself across the floor, reaching out with the Cosmic Hand. Searching, grabbing!

I feel power—undefined, unknown—coursing through it. And with that hand and what I find with it, I'm able to reach every monster on board—all the way to the parking garage and its exit . . .

I open my hand, and the PA microphone clangs to the broken floor. That's all I got.

Ghazt whimpers: a squeak so soft I barely hear it. "Shhh . . ." Thrull says cruelly, tightening the bone-whip until Ghazt goes silent. Then—

FA-SHINK!

Ghazt falls as Thrull's bone-whip snaps straight, a long blade pressed to my throat.

Thrull's voice is a ragged snarl. "You didn't even try to reach your weapon. For someone who caused me so much trouble, I expected more. Did you expect more, too? I think you did. Fear not—there is more to come. You see, Jack . . ."

I WILL END YOU NOW. YOU, THE BOY, WILL FALL. BUT YOUR SKELETON WILL RISE BY MY HAND. AND THEN, I WILL USE YOU TO DESTROY YOUR FRIENDS, DOWN TO THE LAST.

I swallow.

And then I hear a voice.

"Stop where you are, Thrull."

Huh? Who just said that? I look up—and my mouth falls open and my eyes go wide.

It's Johnny Steve. And he's not alone. At every level of the mall, monsters are stepping toward the railings.

I'm confused. Scared. They should be gone. They were supposed to have escaped! If we didn't buy them time, didn't save them, then this has all been for nothing.

But then I see that their arms are full. They're holding loot, all of them: water pistols, Wiffle balls, buckets.

All of it dripping with Ultra-Slime, and all of it aimed at Thrull.

"This is us working together," one monster says.

"This is us fighting back," says another.

Thrull looks up. His left leg buckles, then goes stiff again. It's a quick thing, and if he hadn't corrected it so quickly, I wouldn't have noticed.

But it's clear: he's hurt, too. Drops of Ultra-Slime drip down his arm and pool at his feet.

And whatever Thrull wants from Ghazt, I'm guessing he needs Ghazt alive. That means Ghazt is a (just barely) living ticking clock.

Without the monsters' return, Thrull would have ended me. And probably June.

But now . . .

Thrull's eyes scan the monsters above.

His eyes turn to me—staring hard. It's not just a promise that he'll see me again—that's kind of a given. This is more than that . . .

Thanks to the Cosmic Hand, I am tied forever to the future of this fight. I can never bow out, can never just quit. Even if I wanted to.

And I have a feeling Thrull is thinking something similar—like our fates are now intertwined.

Cosmic Hand or not, Thrull will never let up. He won't quit until he has destroyed *me*, Jack Sullivan, the dopey kid who can never quite get it over on him, can never quite defeat him, but remains a post-apocalyptic thorn in his side nonetheless . . .

Nope. Thrull's not gonna be satisfied until I'm dead.

With a snapping crack, he yanks Ghazt upward— hoisting the massive rat body over his shoulder.

Thrull turns. A raspy, pained yelp falls from Ghazt's lips as Thrull stomps out. And then, with one final swing of the bone-whip, Thrull smashes the pillar holding up Evie and Ghazt's Food Court headquarters. It collapses in a heap of rubble.

And when the smoke and dust clear, Thrull is gone . . . and Ghazt is gone with him.

chapter twenty-five

The next attack comes from behind. It's a hug attack, courtesy, June Del Toro.

She's tackling me, flipping over me, flopping on to the floor.

"Is that what you call that?" I ask.

June sits up, half giggling. "Hey, better than a kinda-sorta defeat. I mean, we lived, Evie fled, Ghazt is toast, and now we have thousands of monsters who are willing to *fight*!"

She's right about all of that, and I'm definitely happy, but . . . "It also sounds like Thrull is gonna try to get some information out of Ghazt. To do something. Which seems . . . not great?"

"Shh," June says. "Just let me have this. Let all of us have this. Including *you*."

"The mayor declares this a day of partying!" Johnny Steve shouts. He's waving a two-liter bottle of grape soda and foam is flying everywhere. That gets me giggling right along with June.

"Johnny Steve, your campaign manager is in one hundred percent agreement," June says. "Now, where are Dirk and Quint? I wanna get the actual, non–Victory Geyser party started *now*."

And I realize I have no idea. They should be here, celebrating with us, right now. That's how we always end these adventures! Why aren't they?

A voice suddenly speaks up—tired and raspy. "Quint's conjurer's cane . . . Something . . ."

It's Yursl, slowly shuffling toward us. She

looks near collapse. "Something went wrong . . ."

The blood drains from June's face. "What?"

My heart starts pounding hard and my legs feel weak—too weak to stand, so I'm grateful when June rises, helping me up, leading me outside, to the rear of the mall, the place Quint and Dirk were last headed.

But when I see what's there, I'm ready to sit down again. We're staring at a smoldering hole in the earth. Lying in the hole is the rear half of the Bone Howler. It has been perfectly sliced in two. The front half of its body? It's not there.

Just . . . gone.

And so are Quint and Dirk.

I sink to the ground.

I look around, desperate to see Quint pop out from behind a rock, yelling "Gotcha!" Or Dirk leaping up, laughing, saying, "Look how scared they were!"

But that doesn't happen.

I don't see my friends. I don't see Thrull or his army or any of that.

I do see Evie, though. In the far distance, on my BoomKart. She's speeding away—off to who knows where . . .

I look up at June, hoping she'll have something reassuring to say. She doesn't. She looks too gut-punched to say anything.

She just takes my hand.

And we stay there, waiting for our friends to come back.

We stay there for a long time.

TO BE CONTINUED IN SPRING 2022!

Acknowledgments

This was the most difficult book yet—and I'm tremendously grateful to so many people. Dana Leydig and Leila Sales, for helping me find my way. Douglas Holgate and Jim Hoover, of course. Jennifer Dee, for keeping me busy. Josh Pruett and Haley Mancini, for being smart and funny. And my endless thanks to Felicia Frazier, Debra Polansky, Joe English, Todd Jones, Mary McGrath, Abigail Powers, Krista Ahlberg, Marinda Valenti, Sola Akinlana, Mia Alberro, Emily Romero, Elyse Marshall, Carmela Iaria, Christina Colangelo, Felicity Vallence, Sarah Moses, Kara Brammer, Alex Garber, Lauren Festa, Michael Hetrick, Trevor Ingerson, Rachel Wease, Lyana Salcedo, Kim Ryan, Helen Boomer, and everyone in PYR Sales and PYR Audio. Ken Wright, more than ever. Dan Lazar, Cecilia de la Campa, Alessandra Birch, Torie Doherty-Munro, and everyone at Writers House.

© Ruby Brallier

MAX BRALLIER!

is a *New York Times*, *USA Today*, and *Wall Street Journal* bestselling author. His books and series include the Last Kids on Earth, Eerie Elementary, Mister Shivers, Galactic Hot Dogs, and *Can YOU Survive the Zombie Apocalypse?* He is a writer and producer for Netflix's Emmy Award–winning adaptation of the Last Kids on Earth. Max lives in Los Angeles with his wife and daughter. Visit him at MaxBrallier.com.

DOUGLAS HOLGATE!

(skullduggery.com.au) has been a freelance comic book artist and illustrator based in Melbourne, Australia, for more than ten years. He's illustrated books for publishers such as HarperCollins, Penguin Random House, Hachette, and Simon & Schuster, including the Planet Tad series, Cheesie Mack, Case File 13, and *Zoo Sleepover*. Douglas has illustrated comics for Image, Dynamite, Abrams, and Penguin Random House. He's currently working on the self-published series Maralinga, which received grant funding from the Australian Society of Authors and the Victorian Council for the Arts, as well as the all-ages graphic novel *Clem Hetherington and the Ironwood Race*, published by Scholastic Graphix, both co-created with writer Jen Breach. Follow Douglas on Twitter @douglasbot.